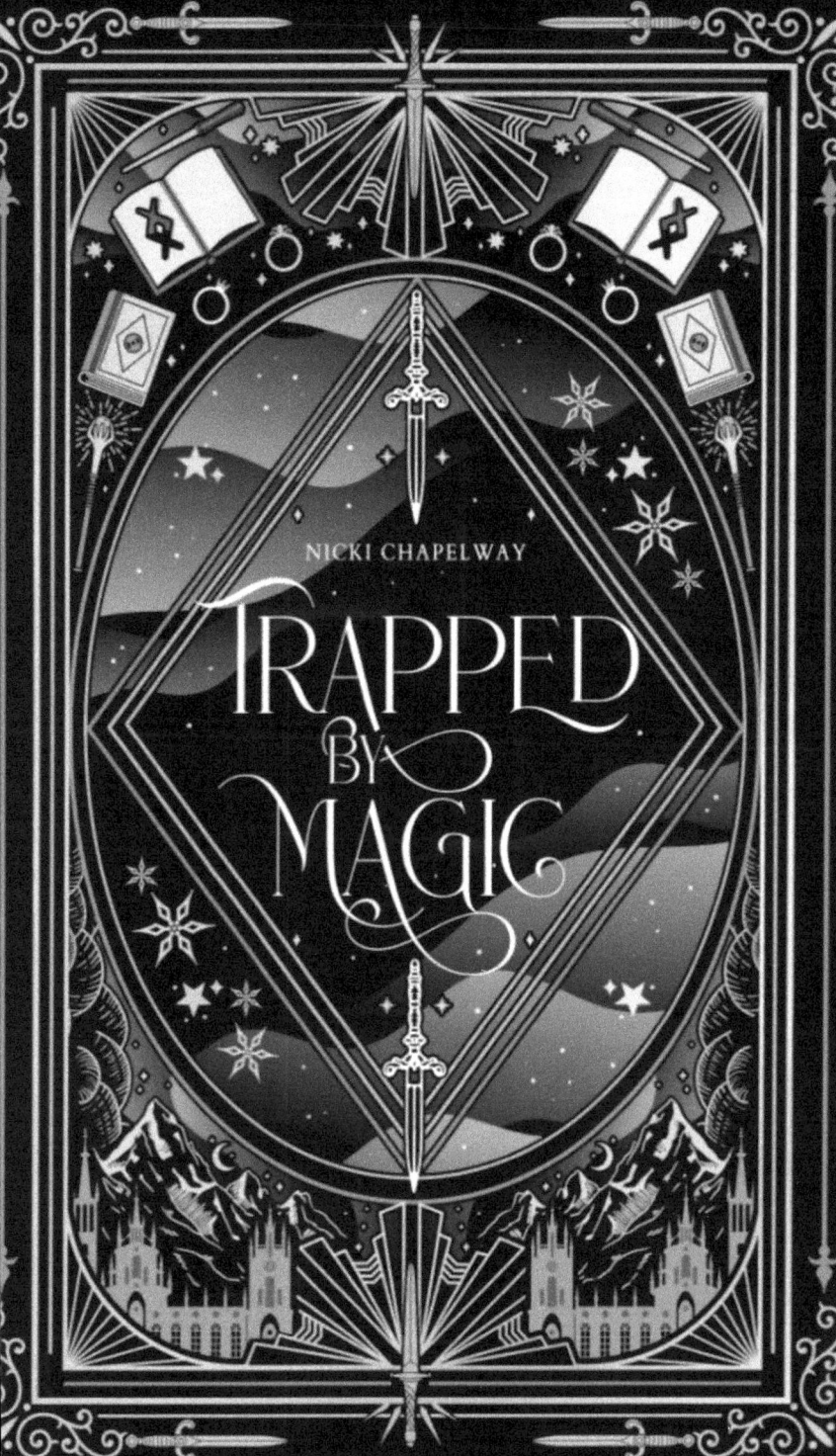

NICKI CHAPELWAY

TRAPPED BY MAGIC

TRAPPED BY MAGIC
OF SEAS AND TIDES BOOK TWO
NICKI CHAPELWAY

DRAGONFLIGHT PRESS

CONTENTS

Copyright	IX
Dedication	1
Map	2
	3
	4
1. Chapter One	5
	16
2. Chapter Two	17
	22
3. Chapter Three	23
	30
4. Chapter Four	31
	36

5.	Chapter Five	37
		44
6.	Chapter Six	45
		52
7.	Chapter Seven	53
		58
8.	Chapter Eight	59
		66
9.	Chapter Nine	67
		74
10.	Chapter Ten	75
		82
11.	Chapter Eleven	83
		88
12.	Chapter Twelve	89
		96
13.	Chapter Thirteen	97
		102
14.	Chapter Fourteen	103

15. Chapter Fifteen — 113
16. Chapter Sixteen — 123
17. Chapter Seventeen — 129
18. Chapter Eighteen — 137
19. Chapter Nineteen — 145
20. Chapter Twenty — 157
21. Chapter Twenty-One — 167
22. Chapter Twenty-Two — 177
23. Chapter Twenty-Three — 185

24.	Chapter Twenty-Four	193
		200
25.	Chapter Twenty-Five	201
		206
26.	Chapter Twenty-Six	207
		212
27.	Chapter Twenty-Seven	213
Epilogue		218
Afterword		222
		223
More Stories from Ruskhazar		224
		225
Also by Nicki Chapelway		227
Of Seas and Tides		229
		230

Copyright © 2024 by Nicki Chapelway

All rights reserved.

No portion of this book may be reproduced in any form without written permission from the publisher or author, except as permitted by U.S. copyright law.

Cover by @saintjupit3rgr4phic

Under the dust jacket art by Lauren Richelue

Map by Nicki Chapelway

Edited by Wisteria Editing

Formatted by Jes Drew

To Uncle Jay and Aunt Lori.
Love you guys a ton!

KA

THE SPICE ISLANDS

VATN OCEAN

RUSKH...
Acc
Ma

RUSKHAZAR
SEA
ELF RUINS
EINAN
Reglagrad
ELLEF
SEA
N
DESERTS
Chaim 2021

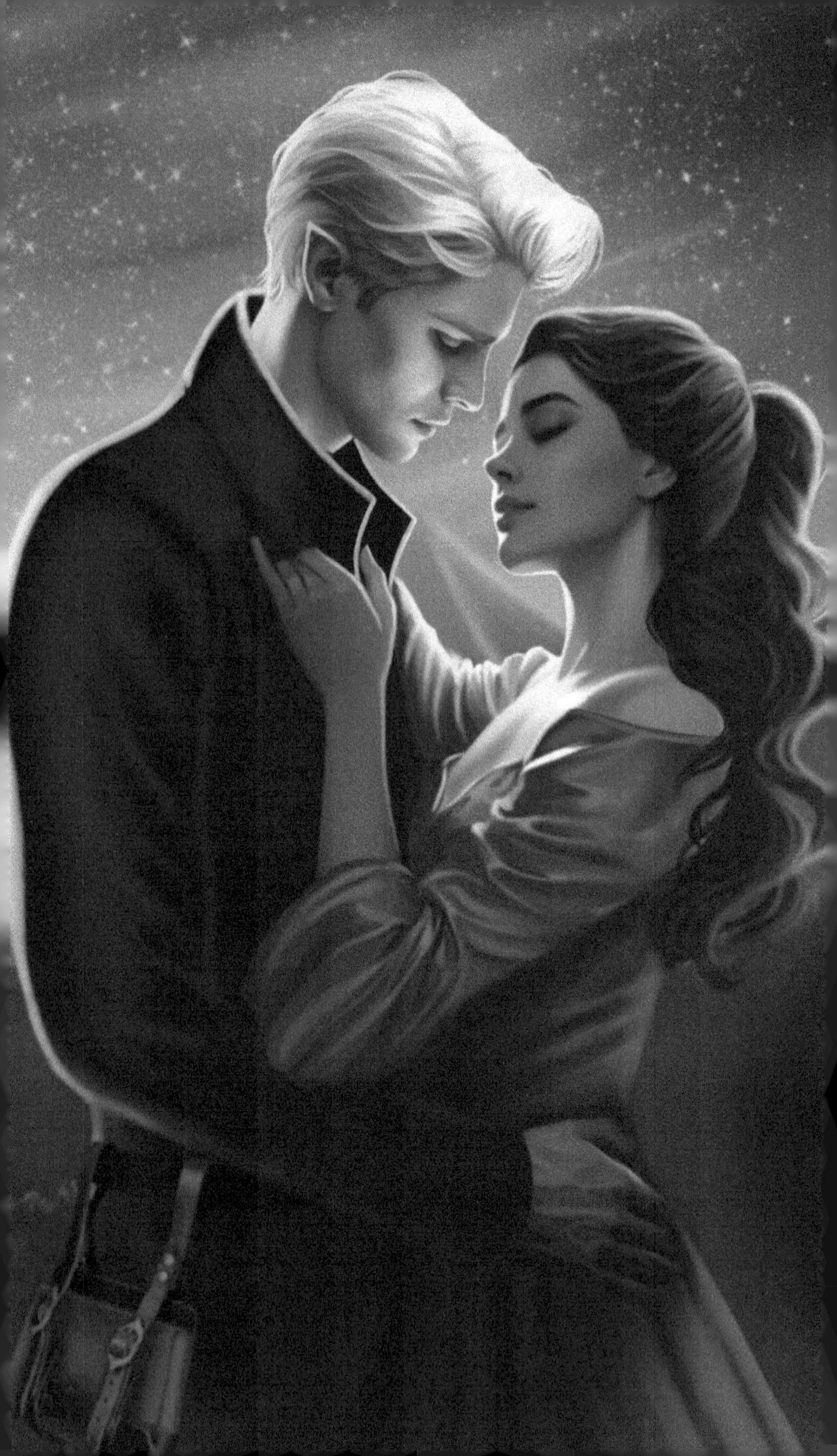

CHAPTER ONE
BRONWYN

Year 26 of the Third Era

If it had been solely up to me, I never would have allowed something as powerful and dangerous as magic to be so easily accessible.

All one needs to attend the Academy of Magickers is a little bit of magical proficiency—something that three of the four people groups native to Ruskhazar are capable of.

Magic itself is no easy skill to hone, despite how many people are born with it in their blood. Indeed, it takes many years to even become remotely proficient at it. Spells are difficult to memorize and cantankerous like our cook's poison recipes; the slightest variation from the norm could have disastrous consequences. Most people need magic enhancers such as staffs and wands to aid them in using it. Only the most powerful family bloodlines can wield magic in its raw form.

And yet, anyone can attend the Academy of Magickers where they will have every resource needed to excel at magic practically at their fingertips. Whether they deserve to have it or not.

Perhaps it is my father's teachings, but power is something that should be sought by few and attained by even fewer.

After all, if everyone is equally powerful then no one is powerful. What is power if not an edge over your enemy?

Now, don't get me wrong, it isn't as if I think I'm better than everyone else. Quite the opposite actually, I know that I am one of the many who has no right to learn magic. I am well aware of where I hail from. By blood, I'm nothing more than a farmer's daughter. I was born to work the ground, not study magic in illustrious halls.

By all rights, I should be a nobody, just like my birth father was.

But that was not what the gods had in store for me and my sister. I don't know what caused us to catch Elwis the Eel's eye, but he chose us all the same. He chose to make us a part of his family, to call us daughters, and raise us up to a position above that of a farmer's daughter.

I don't remember much about my life before Elwis took us in, but I do remember the fear. And I still have a scar or two from the beatings.

But I'm a farmer's daughter no longer. Elwis saved me from that life by killing the man I called "father," and he didn't abandon me and my twin Natasya. No, he took us in as his own daughters. Through Elwis, perhaps, I am a little more deserving of this academy and the pursuit of magic. After all, my father is wealthy and capable of buying me any magical trinket my heart could desire.

But because of Elwis I can never be a mere magicker. I am the daughter of who might just be the most powerful man in Ruskhazar—not that anyone would realize it.

I glance at the walls around me, stained windows paint a pretty picture but also blot out the natural light of the sun. These hallowed and ancient halls offer a welcoming air, promising learning and mastery of magic to all that would seek to attain it.

The Sanctuary of the Seeker reads engraved in letters etched into the stone above the arched door that leads to the spiral staircase that would take me to the second floor.

All who come to the Academy to learn magic are welcome. It's a foolish policy, one that allows a crime lord's daughter to just walk through its doors.

I draw to a halt however when I catch sight of a flash of silver hair followed by an annoyingly sultry laugh. I curl my hand into a fist, grinding my teeth together as I take in the young man leaning against the base of the stairwell.

My father controls the mining and farming industries. What land he does not own is owned by his friends. Those in the council of notability seek his advice before they make a stand on issues. From the outside, he is a powerful, influential, and wealthy merchant. He is a good friend to have, and thus, he has many friends.

However, Elwis doesn't just rule the business and political sphere; under the surface, he is also the head of one of the most powerful assassin guilds there are. He also runs a ring of thieves and has the entire criminal underworld in a chokehold.

Which is why it is so difficult for me to keep my face stoic as I face my first-year tormentor. Wilder Zubkov.

Outwardly, Wilder has it all: family name, wealth, prestige. He is from a powerful magical bloodline; his family requires no magical trinkets to be formidable magickers. Not that his family spares any expense. After all, what is power if it cannot be enhanced?

To top it all off, he is handsome. The sort of handsomeness that allows him to get away with just about anything. When he looks at an unwitting victim with those dark eyes and gives a small smile, he is capable of melting the heart of even the most stoic professor.

While I hold some sway due to my adopted father's name, that sort of thing doesn't matter to someone like

Wilder. Bloodline is everything, and unfortunately, my bloodline leads back to an abusive farmer I would rather have nothing to do with.

And so, Wilder has made it his life mission to make certain that I know I'm not welcomed here at the academy. If his mocking words making fun of my heritage and belittling Elwis's position weren't enough, he also hides my stuff. Conveniently, snakes find their way into my room. Somehow the professors—colleagues of Wilder's father—give me poor grades when I know I answered correctly.

It is a good thing that I learned to never look at an outward appearance; otherwise, I would have missed the fact that Wilder Zubkov is a vile, reprehensible toad with a fat ego and an annoying laugh.

I wasn't prepared for the anger that would course through my veins when I saw him again. His *antics* made my last year utterly miserable. I had to spend my entire break convincing myself that I was a better person, and I did not need to have my father assassinate his entire family. It had been difficult, but with all the distance, I was able to fool myself into believing I was a good person.

But here is Wilder standing there again with that arrogant smirk as he looks me over. "It seems that we are just letting anyone in here now. Even Eels."

Even though Eel is actually my name, since I took the name of the man who raised me, I bristle whenever I hear it come from Wilder.

I know that I shouldn't stop. I should just keep walking and pretend that I didn't hear him, escape to my room or a quiet corner of the library, and lose myself in a book. Instead, my boot scrapes to stone floor of the academy, a facility that is as large as a city, built entirely from ancient magic and massive stonework thus earning it the title "the city of stone".

I jut my chin as I draw to a halt right in front of him and two or three of his snickering imbecilic friends. "It must be a difficult concept for you to grasp," I say, tilting my head. "To have a loving father. Someone you would actually want to carry the name of. But I wish you the best in trying to wrap your mind around that concept."

I know it's a low blow, the sort of jab that Wilder would make, but my father always taught me to fight by turning my enemy's weapons against them. To be frank, if Wilder were not such a horrible creature, I might even pity him. His strained relationship with his father is no secret. After all, his father is a powerful and cunning magicker, a prominent name in the academy, and he expects his son to continue the family legacy of meddling in the magical world.

Wilder already has much to redeem himself for in his father's eyes, since he was born of an illicit affair with a servant.

Still, he is Zubkov and so things are expected of him. Doors are opened for him. And he is still his father's son even if neither of them particularly cares for that fact.

"If that is what you have to tell yourself to get through being an inn keeper's daughter."

I snort. It's true, the start of Elwis's empire was the inn that he gifted to my adopted mother Vala, but he was never a humble inn keeper. Around the time my father bought that inn, he was already a member of the assassin Family of Night, and over the years he became their leader, starting his own ring of thieves and becoming a ruler of a criminal empire, all while buying land and betraying business partners.

But, of course, Wilder has no idea of any of this. And so, like any ignorant person, he talks even when he has no idea what he is saying.

I fold my arms, studying the third button on his vest. I don't want to look up into his face because he is and has always been unfortunately handsome, and I have no time to deal with my own treacherous thoughts.

The button is engraved with an owl, it's a fine piece of craftmanship, and displays his family's wealth. Wilder is so rich that he can't even have plain buttons.

Maybe I should have my buttons engraved. Is that what people do to display power these days? Maybe it can finally earn me some respect around here.

Since Elwis is virtually immortal as both a Lower Elf and a vampire, I don't ever expect to inherit the business from him, but I will hold a place in power within it alongside my father. He has already been training me and my sisters to be ready. I am to be the magicker of the family.

I will be a somebody and Wilder will only ever remain a *nobody*.

But I can't say any of this because keeping my father's secret is paramount. The whole world believes he is a reputable businessman, and I will not be the daughter who betrays his secret.

I force a smile. "Anyway, as lovely as it was to see you again, Wilder, I would rather set myself aflame and slowly burn to death than talk to you any longer, so I think I'll be off."

I start to turn to leave, but just then he reaches up and snags my hair. I stiffen as he gives it a slight tug. It doesn't even hurt, but it's enough to boil my blood.

I have always had thick unruly hair; it falls half in cascading waves and half as tangled curls, and I have spent much of my life attempting to tame it. It is long and thick, and the slightest bit of moisture will cause it to become a frizzy mess.

My twin has hair much like mine, but she was blessed to have red hair which was always meant to be a bit wild. My hair is a dull color of brown and has always been a sensitive issue for me.

I do *not* appreciate Wilder having the audacity to lay his hands on it. Why if my father knew he would slice off each of his fingers. One by bloody one.

I whirl, balling my hands into fists ready to give Wilder a piece of my mind, but I freeze as I finally look him in the face.

Wilder has always been quite pale, a fact that is emphasized by his stark white hair, a token of his higher elf descent. He has always looked every bit the part of the aristocrat he is with his refined cheekbones and haughty brow, but there is something about his appearance that has a sharper look now. His jawline is more angled, his face narrower.

And his eyes... his eyes sparkle like twin flames. Like two rubies set in his face.

He smiles, his eyes flicking over me as he waits for my explosion. I think he lives for the moments when I go off on him. It must make him feel so superior that he is able to control his emotions, and I always explode with anger.

But I am frozen.

Slowly, I watch that smile slide off his face, but I can't seem to move or stop myself from staring.

Many have convinced themselves that vampires are nothing more than bedtime stories, told to children to keep them in their beds at night. Despite the numerous accounts of their existence, most people are content to believe that monsters existed only in the past, long ago wiped out by our bold ancestors.

Those that would acknowledge that vampires even exist choose to see them as wretched creatures. Things that are barely even human that hide from the sun and forget that they are not animals as they rot away in deep caves.

It is true that there are savage vampires, animalistic creatures that are nothing but instinct and bloodlust.

It's true that long ago the monsters were nearly wiped out, but what these people don't seem to realize is that as long as there are humans, there are vampires because any human is capable of becoming one.

And they forget that these vampires were at first humans.

So, no one thinks to look for them in society. No one expects a vampire to tell them good morning, or perhaps to tug on their ponytail while mocking their family name.

They expect vampires to rip out people's throats and hiss in the daylight.

I happen to be an expert on vampires. After all, I was raised by one.

I know a vampire when I see one, even if others would be willing to overlook the slight changes to a person's appearance.

And this year there is something different about Wilder Zubkov. This year, he's a vampire.

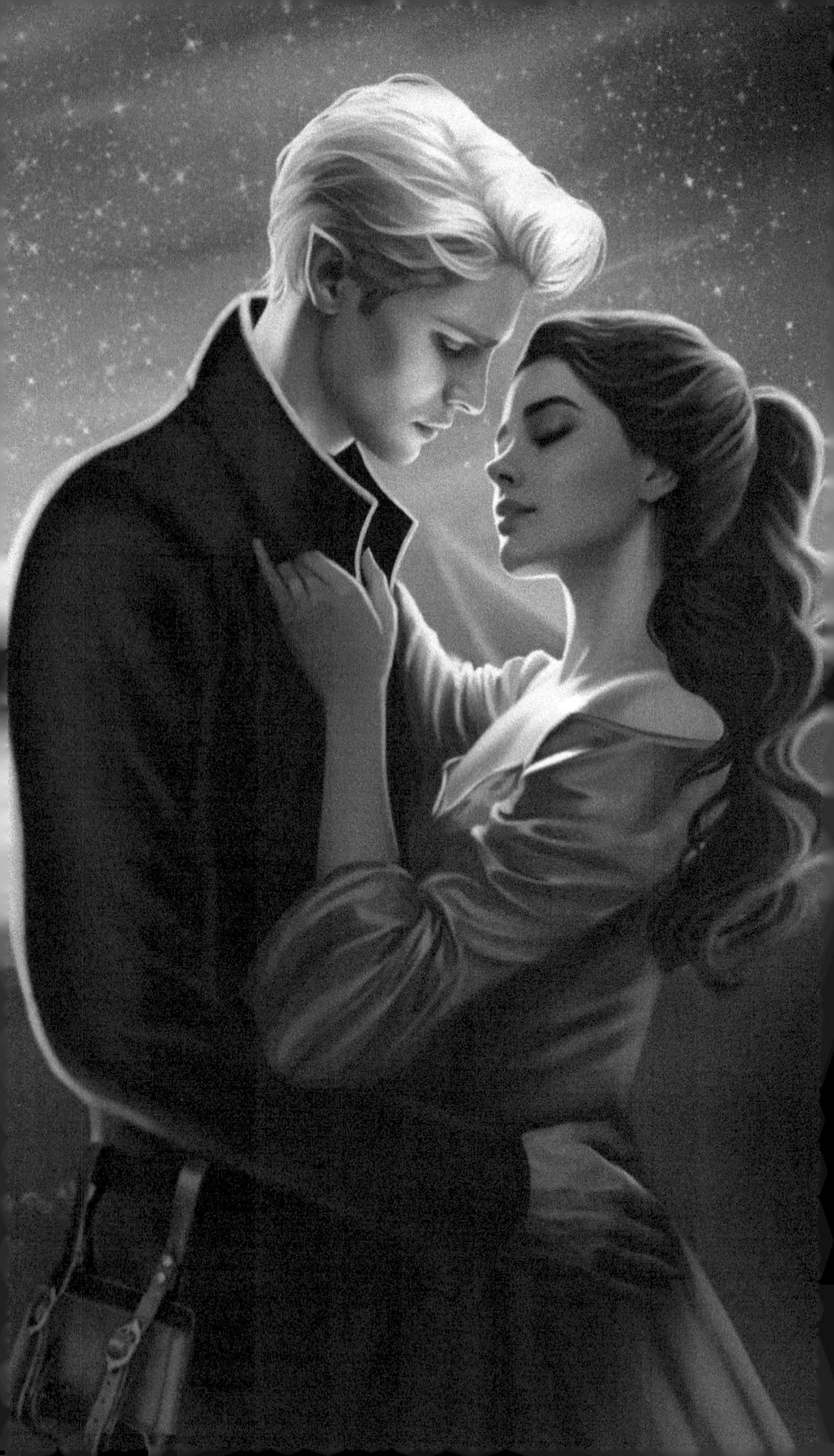

CHAPTER TWO
WILDER

If I had blood still pumping in my veins, I think I would feel it drain from my face as Bronwyn continues to stare at me.

Emotions play across her enchanting hazel eyes. First shock, then realization, then intrigue. Finally, she blinks and turns away. She reaches up to tuck a strand of hair behind her ear, looks like she is about to say something, but instead snaps her mouth shut and scurries off up the stairs.

And leaves me standing there with a sense of dread pooling in my stomach.

She knows.

I don't know how or even just what, but that girl knows something, and it scares me to no end that she does.

"What was that?" Asimov, one of the people that I have loosely ascribed the title of *friend*, asks with a laugh. "She looked like she saw a ghost."

I force a smile as I turn to him, trying my best to mask my panic. Fortunately, I have a lot of practice doing that since it is what I do every time I am around my father. "I have heard that ghosts occasionally roam these halls."

As of now, Asimov does not know of my *altered* state, and I cannot allow him to catch on. Not until I decide what to do with him.

"Are you referring to the murdered students?" Gregos, another student from a prestigious family who I have been ordered to keep in the good graces of, asks with disdainful snort. "I thought that whole sordid affair was over now that the professor that killed them was stopped."

"How could the affair just be over? They didn't come back from the dead, Gregos," I reply stiffly. "Last I checked, they were still murdered and possibly tormented spirits."

Maybe they found their way to Skyhold, or maybe they still haunt these halls. I wonder what they think of me being here, would they recognize a fellow member of the undead?

Are they even aware enough to notice?

It's a sad state of affairs to even be undead, but I think it is even sadder to know that I'm not the only undead creature here. It is quite telling about the state of our world when the deceased are no longer allowed to rest in peace.

There's a lot of conjecture on just what a vampire is and what even causes this unique state. Some say a curse, some say a blessing, others say it's a disease. But all agree that a vampire is no longer quite a human. *Monster.* That is what they call vampires. That is what they would call me if they knew, and would they be necessarily wrong?

No, I think not.

So, while my soul was not ripped away from my body only to have it be resurrected like the common undead, I would say that the term still very much applies. After all, my soul was ripped away from my humanity.

Fortunately for me, vampires are largely misconceived, and up until this very moment, I have managed to move largely undiscovered despite my previous misgivings.

But I suppose that has all changed now because with just one look, Bronwyn figured me out. I'm certain of it, I saw the look in her eyes as she stared into mine.

She knows I'm a vampire. I don't know how. I don't know what I did wrong, but now I'm worried that in one day I have foiled all of my father's plans.

I swallow past my dry throat. I hope that I will grow accustomed to this thirst that can only be quenched by blood. It is nice not necessarily needing to eat or sleep, but I'm not sure if I would consider trading that with a dependence on blood as particularly an upgrade.

I ball my hand into a fist as I turn back to Gregos, painting a smile across my face. "But we are second years now. That no account Eel shouldn't take up another second of our time."

I have a more important task to focus my time on.

Gregos folds his arms. "I still think we should incinerate her belongings. That should give her the message that we don't want common stock in our school."

I reach up, running a hand through my hair. "Speaking of common stock, do you know which of the families will have students here this year? Are there any new first years we should befriend?"

Gregos's mouth twists and he seems to completely forget about Bronwyn the Eel as he considers my question. "I'm unsure yet; give me a day or so to actually get a feel of what is going on at this Academy. We were just on break, you know? You can't exactly expect me to bounce back so quickly. I'm still half inebriated from last night's celebrations."

I release a frustrated sigh. Gregos might think that I am only pretending to be this upset. He doesn't know how high the stakes are. "What's the point of even keeping you around for?" I grumble under my breath; although, it's loud enough for him to hear.

Gregos laughs clearly not reading me correctly, but then, what else is new? We have only ever been associates because of our fathers, not because of common interest or even because I can stand the man. Although, he would claim that we are the closest of friends.

"Lighten up Zubkov," Asimov says with a slap on my shoulder. "This is going to be our year, and nothing can stand in the way of that."

See I know that isn't going to be true because I know things that Asimov does not. This will be no one's year, at least no one living's. I have half the mind to tell him that, but I know that doing so would mean that I'd have to reveal my vampiric state and my new unholy mission. And I am unsure if I am willing to tell them just yet.

While I am at the liberty of choosing new vampire recruits at my discretion, I don't know if Gregos and Asimov would make the list. Not just because of how I fear they would use the power, but also because they are the closest things to friends that I have ever had despite my loathing of them, and I'm not entirely sure if I am quite ready to share my curse with someone who I would even remotely consider a friend.

None of that will matter though if Bronwyn the Eel can't keep her mouth shut.

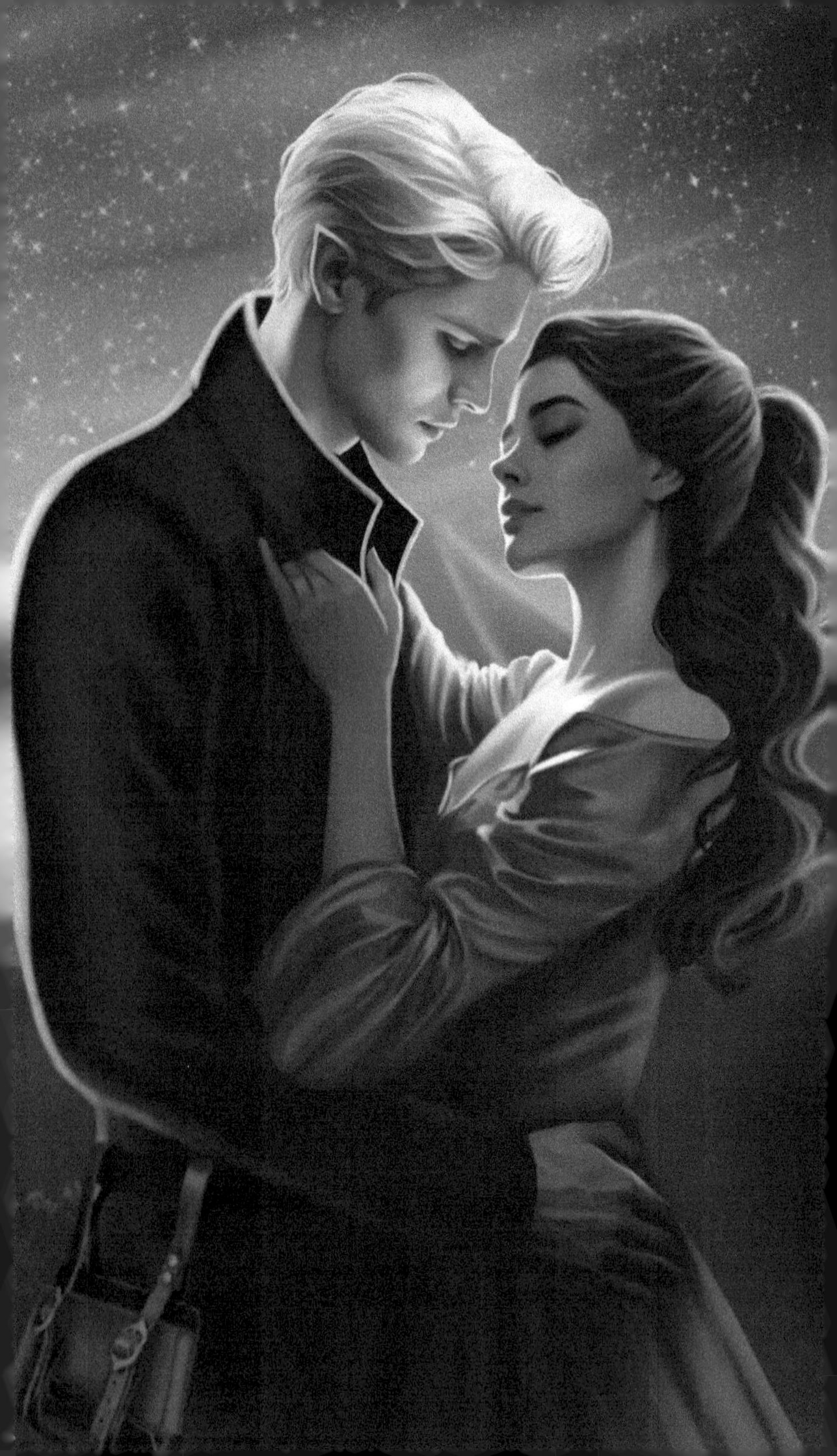

CHAPTER THREE
BRONWYN

I have no real friends at the Academy. I suppose it would be hard to make friends under these false pretenses. Not that I need friends. If I need someone to complain to about Wilder, I can simply write home to my sister, and if I need company, I have the thousands of books found in libraries scattered across the Academy to provide that.

And so I head to the library. My belongings were sent ahead so I traveled lightly to get here, and I can go to my room to freshen up after I've worked through my muddled, twisted thoughts.

Jetting curse Wilder how does he always managed to have this effect on me? I had convinced myself— foolishly I know— that perhaps after I had some time away, I'd have been able to get all Wilder's twisted words out of my head and be able to focus on my mission.

What does it matter if that boy thinks I'm good enough or not? I do not find my worth in him. I am the daughter of the most powerful crime lord to walk through Ruskhazar now, and perhaps ever. What some aristocrat thinks of me should not matter in the slightest. It shouldn't even make it to a second thought, and yet, his words ring in my head.

I release a frustrated growl as I enter the library. I'm relieved to see that I am alone with just these books. The books at least cannot judge me, that's why I prefer their company to that of my peers.

See, this is my problem. This is why I even have to come back to this school. I should have accomplished my mission in my first year. The gods know that father was expecting me not to come back home empty handed after spending a whole year here. And yet, I'm no closer to my goal than I was when I was entering the city of stone for the first time, gaping wide-eyed at the massive architecture and impressive structure that had been built purely by magic.

If I was fair to myself, I would say that Wilder certainly was an unexpected obstacle. Never in my wildest dreams would I have expected someone like him to make it his life's mission to make someone like me experience a living Skyhold. Still with all that I have been through and who my father is, I should have been able to overcome this issue without any problems. And yet, here I am back at the Academy in my second year and is already starting up again.

However, if I was being truly brutally honest, I would have to admit that Wilder is only a welcome excuse for why I haven't been able to accomplish my mission, and that is simply because I'm not ready to leave the Academy. I love my family; do not get me wrong. I love my sisters. I adore my mother, and I practically worship the ground on which my father walks. But while none of them would ever try to make me feel like I don't belong, it is true that there is a part of me that feels as if I am an outsider.

Everyone in my family is driven to the point of obsession. Father has his empire to run; mother has her inn, Natasya has her dead things to play with, and Coraline spends so much time in solitude that it seems almost as if it is her own pursuit. I have always felt the odd one out with only measured interest in anything. That is until I entered the Academy, and I found these books, learned the spells, and I smell the pure and unfettered magic. It was only then that I found myself wondering if the life of running a crime family alongside my father was the life that I wanted? Or did I perhaps crave something a bit more scholarly?

There would be many limitations as my father's personal Magicker, for one he does not think I should have to graduate for the position like anyone else in the Academy of Magickers. As a sorcerer who practices in secret, he believes in learning for yourself rather than standing on the knowledge of intellectual giants. He only needs someone to read a spellbook, not a person to discover new spells and forge into unheard of fields of magic.

I shake my head. It is a betrayal to my family to even think this. What am I thinking? I belong to a great family with that great comes the responsibility of maintaining that greatness.

I will never regret not growing up as a farmer's daughter, but sometimes I wonder that if I had would the expectation of what I should do be quite so crushing.

Or would I have been able to be free to pursue this niggling ideal, a dream just waiting to be born. A hope waiting with bated breath to see if it can live.

No. I almost laugh at the foolish thought. Of course not. Because if I was a farmer's daughter, I'd be working the ground to pay off a lord, barely scraping by, and certainly not free to do whatever I want.

See that's the thing, isn't it? There's always something taking away your freedom.

Family, expectations, money, station. Whatever it is, those things live to crush dreams. I've allowed that hope to hold its breath, waiting in a place of stasis for a year now.

I'm back at the academy because I didn't steal a book when I could have. All because I wanted to come back. It has nothing to do with Wilder at all.

I'm not sure if Elwis believed my excuses when I returned home on break after my first-year empty handed, but I doubt that even he would have thought of the true reasoning behind my failure. And my father has made a career out of thinking the worst of people. After all, no one can stab you in the back if you never give them your back. He just never thought to do that to his family.

We are his one and true weakness, and I never intend to allow it to be exploited.

No, there shall be no further dallying, no distractions—no matter how tempting these books are— until I get the book that I actually came here for.

The spellbook of Petrov Hansimov, better known as the last lord of the sea. He was the only lord of the sea as far as I know, but for some reason *last* stuck to his title.

After all, not many magickers are clamoring to learn spells to control the raging waves when we live inland, surrounded by a ring of mountains that completely block us off from a sea that is hundreds of miles away.

Still, if my father wants that spellbook he shall have it. And nothing will stand in my way this year.

Although there is the matter of Wilder now being a vampire, that may warrant a little distraction.

As I stride toward the door, ready to leave the solitude of the library my eye snags on a beautiful spine etched with golden filigree. It's too pretty to just walk past. My hand snags out, pulling it out. Followed by the three books right next to it.

To be fair, I doubt my father's empire would crumble if I read a *few* books.

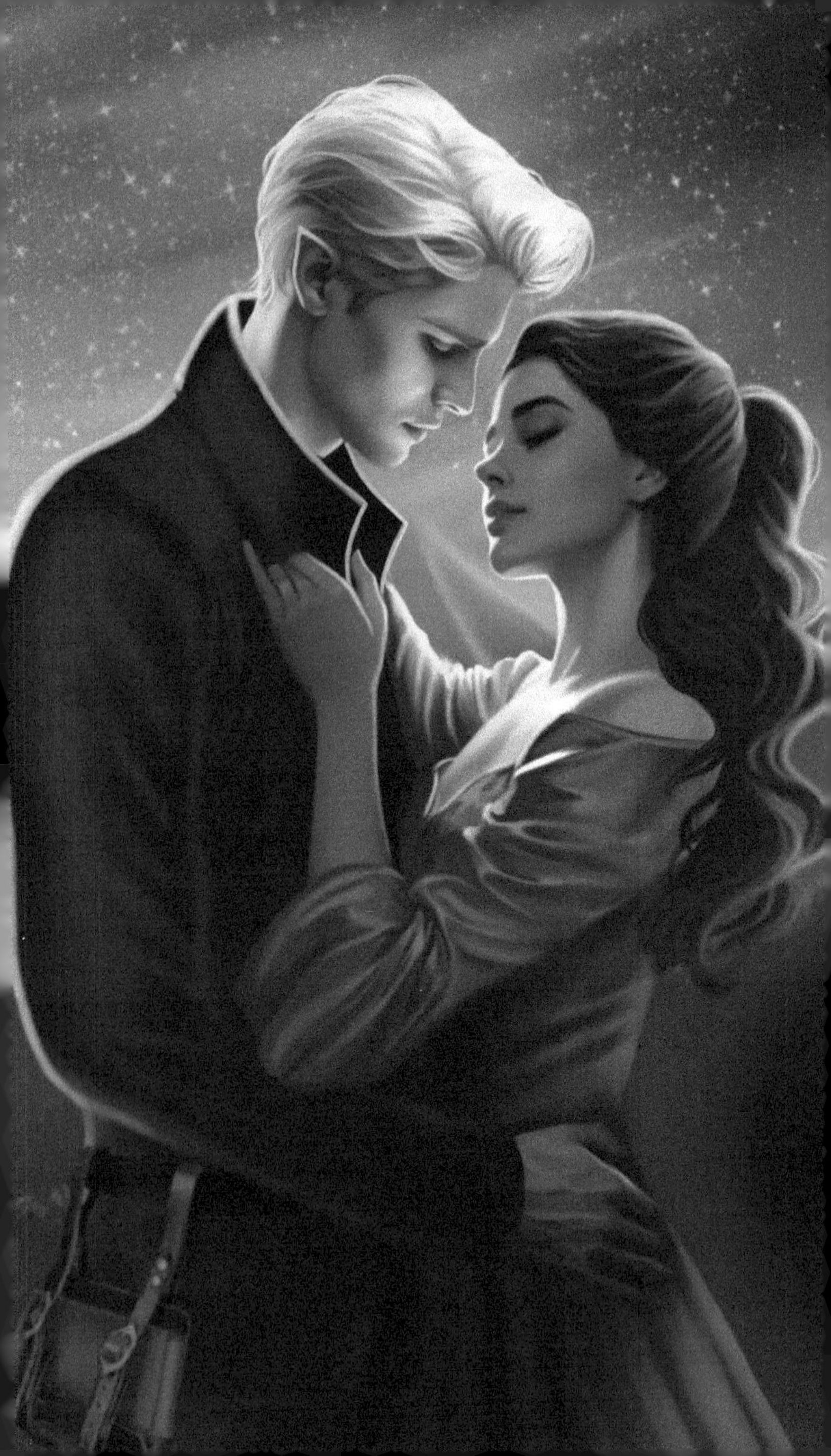

CHAPTER FOUR
WILDER

"You seem distracted."

I blink, turning my attention back to Professor Morozov. As a second-year professor, this is my first time actually under his tutelage. The second-year students and professors and classes are kept in an entirely different building than the first years.

Although I wish that this was only our first meeting, Morozov has been my father's associate for years, and over this past break he became my associate as well.

I wonder if I saw him last year and didn't realize the role he would soon play in my life. I was unaware of the plans he and my father had for me until it was too late. How could I have known?

My father has so many business associates that it makes my head spin to even attempt to keep them straight. Which is probably why I never bothered to pay attention to this professor. After all, my father knows many people of prominence within this academy. It's one of the perks of being its primary benefactor.

My father, alongside other nobles with more money than they know to do with, pay for the academy to be able to keep running and capable of taking in students without fee or charge. In return, they get a special commendation from the king and enough moral superiority to sink a ship.

The professor reaches up, rubbing at the bridge of his nose and then mutters in a falsely patient tone, "Do pay attention, I only am speaking of your continued existence."

I reach up, playing with my cuffs. I nod, pretending interest and the professor begins speaking again. His words hit my ears like a buzz as my mind slips back to that hallway, to a moment frozen in time. To Bronwyn's sparking gaze and barely suppressed rage. Her skin flushed with the blood pumping through her veins. So very *alive*. Tan, imperfect, a merchant's daughter, but alive.

Which makes her better than me.

I turn my hand, studying my fingernail. My skin is nearly as pale as the small knicks on my nails. My mother always said that white marks on your nails mean that you have a liar's soul. I think she just said that because my father had them, but maybe it was a saying amongst her people. I can't very well ask her anymore.

"Are you even listening to me, *boy*?"

I blink and look up which seems to give Morozov the answer that he is looking for. He lets out a growl snapping his teeth together. I catch a flash of his fangs before he presses his lips together into a thin line changing from a monster to a tired looking professor in the blink of an eye. "Need I remind you of the importance of our mission? It hinges upon not only secrecy but all our abilities to play our parts."

I nod even though I'm only half listening again. I've heard this all from my father. This importance is why he justified forcing me to become a vampire. I'm still not entirely sure if I want the same thing he wants.

After all, it is for a greater freedom for vampires that we are doing this. I never would have cared about such a thing if I had not been forced to become a vampire myself over the last few months.

It seems to me that if this mission hadn't existed at all, I'd be in a better place. But now that I'm here, I have no choice but to succeed. With my father, failure has never been an option, and now that I'm working with Morozov, I doubt that the professor will take any more kindly to it.

But the secrecy bit I do find troubling.

What am I to do about Bronwyn, hmm?

When I first entered the academy, I was worried that my changed state would draw too much attention. I knew that vampires have been living in the academy unnoticed, Morozov for one. But when even the people who could even be remotely considered friends didn't notice, I was starting to feel more comfortable as a vampire.

People only see what they expect to see, and no one expects to see a bloodsucking monster from your nightmares in a library at your academy.

But not Bronwyn. She saw through my disguised mortality in a second.

The resentment was replaced by a spark of curiosity. If it wasn't such a dire situation, I would have even maybe appreciated seeing her look at me with something other than animosity. My heart stuttered and not just because of the fear of being found out.

Bronwyn has exceptional eyes, but they are always filled with fury when looking at me. Although I would rather die than admit it, I have always admired her intellectual curiosity. It's a bit flattering to be the focus of it.

If only her knowing didn't threaten all of my father's craftily laid plans. And I know enough about him to know that he, and his business partners would never allow that.

Which leaves me in a precarious situation and Bronwyn in a dangerous one. Because if they learn that she knows, the simplest and easiest solution would be to just make her disappear.

And obviously, I can't allow that to happen; otherwise, who else will glare at me from across the halls with those intelligent eyes?

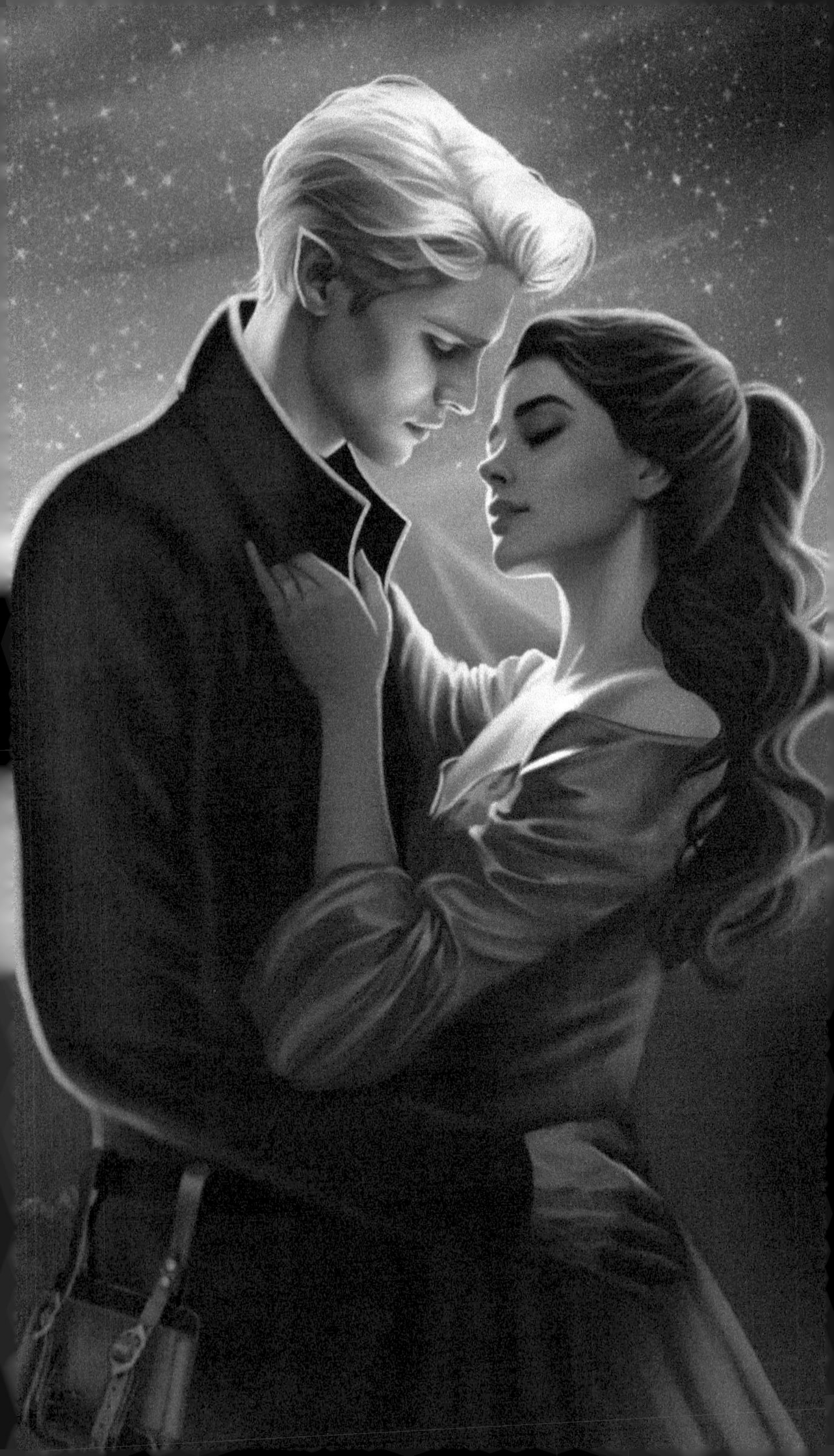

CHAPTER FIVE
BRONWYN

Despite my year spent here with the specific purpose of earning her trust, I still know very little about Sofarynn. I know that she is the custodian of the many libraries here in the Academy of Magickers. She tends to the books and keeps track of where they are and who is currently reading them.

She also has the key to Petrov Hansimov's tomb where his spellbook has been stored since his burial. Occasionally it has been taken out and studied by the Scholar of Spells, which is how I know of its existence, but the academy has done an excellent job at protecting the legacy of one of its illustrious founders.

That tomb, like much in the academy is made with magic. A bombardment couldn't make it in. No, to enter you need a key.

I haven't the finesse for helping myself to belongings that are not mine like my sister Corallin does. She could snatch the soul out of your body without you even realizing. But I'm afraid I have never been quite sneaky or coordinated enough to make it as a pickpocket.

So, when I first came here a year ago, I set out to befriend Sofarynn. If I can figure out what makes her tick, I can figure out what to offer her for her to let me into that tomb.

Money?

Power?

Revenge?

I can get her any of those things. At least, my father can provide it. I just need to know what she wants. Unfortunately, what I have discovered is that Sofarynn is a very private individual. She is quiet, and she keeps to herself.

From her accent and the darker coloring of her skin, I can tell that she hales from the deserts of the south and is not a native of Ruskhazar. She obviously has a great passion for magic and enchanted objects from the care she puts into her duties.

I don't see her really interact with anyone which is why I took to taking my lunch in her office with her. At first, I think she was taken aback and annoyed, but as I walk in today, she looks up expectantly. I catch a hint of a smile before she drops her head.

"You're a bit late," she says, her voice ringing out silky smooth. "I was wondering if you were going to keep this up into the new year."

"And miss the pleasure of your company?" I ask as I slide into the overstuffed chair across from her desk. There are so many books stacked around her desk that I only have a small window to view Sofarynn through as I eat. I unwrap the cloth I bundled my lunch in. Since lunch is usually dried foods such as bread and cheese, it's the meal I choose to eat in here as I try to get into Sofarynn's good graces.

She folds her hands as she studies me, her dark eyes inquisitive. Her ebony dark skin is still smooth and free of wrinkles even though I know that she has been working here for nearly a decade now.

In all that time, she has lived at the academy. I do not know if she has family—she never speaks of them. Even though I'd prefer to keep threats as a last resort, after a year, I still have nothing to exploit.

It's as if she exists only for this academy and the care of these books.

"You look refreshed; did you enjoy your break?" Sofarynn asks, surprising me. I glance up at her swallowing my bread wrong and nearly choking on it. In all my time sitting here eating with her, she rarely says anything past the initial greeting. Normally, I just sit here and eat quietly.

To be honest, for a while, I wasn't even sure if I was allowed in here, and she was just too polite to tell me.

I clear my throat, tapping my hand against my chest. "I did. I spent it with my family." I pull off a piece of bread, but instead of putting it in my mouth, I turn it between my fingers until it starts crumbling.

"Are you very close to your family?"

"I am," I force my hand to go still. Sofarynn might very well not believe me if I don't stop twitching, she may think I'm lying and that could ruin all the progress that I've managed to make. It isn't even a lie. I do love my family with my whole heart. I just don't know what to say to people outside of it. There is so little I can actually share about them. After all, half my family are vampires, necromancers, assassins, and thieves. All things that are heavily frowned upon in society. "My mother is an innkeeper, and my father is a merchant. I have two sisters; one is my twin."

Sofarynn smiles wistfully. "You must miss them when you're here."

"I do," I admit. "It feels as if they are a part of me." My family makes me who I am; I don't even want to know what sort of creature I'd be if Elwis hadn't shown me a father's love.

"I have a brother," Sofarynn admits, glancing down. She twists her fingers as she studies the top of her desk. I force myself to remain still. This is the most she has ever opened up, and I can't scare her by being too over eager. "I love him, but... our paths led us in very different directions. Him to a family. He and his wife have two little girls and a son. They run a wood carving business of all things, in the middle of nowhere," she chuckles. "And here I am, living in the Academy of Magickers."

She doesn't say it, but I know that we both are thinking *alone*.

"Do you speak to your brother often?" I ask after a long moment.

She ducks her head. For a second, I think I have overstepped, that she will withdraw again, but all she does bite down on her lower lip. "No, visiting him brings back painful memories of... what I lost."

I'm about to ask what she means by that, but then she quickly rises from her seat. "Well, look at me prattle on. If I keep you much longer, you will be late for your classes." I glance out the window, taking in the position of the sun and realize that I've actually been here longer than I thought. I jump to my feet.

"Of course!"

"Enjoy your studies," Sofarynn says, that wistful gleam in her eyes again. "You have no idea how fortunate you are. Magic is a gift, cherish it as such."

I give a nod and turn away.

It's a beautiful way of thinking of magic, especially since I know someone like Sofarynn could never wield it. For some reason, magic is something that exists solely in Ruskhazar. Those born outside of it can never wield it.

However, my father's teachings are ingrained too deeply in me. Magic, like anything else, is a commodity.

And I must do what is needed to get my hands on that commodity, even if it means resorting to unlawful means such as theft.

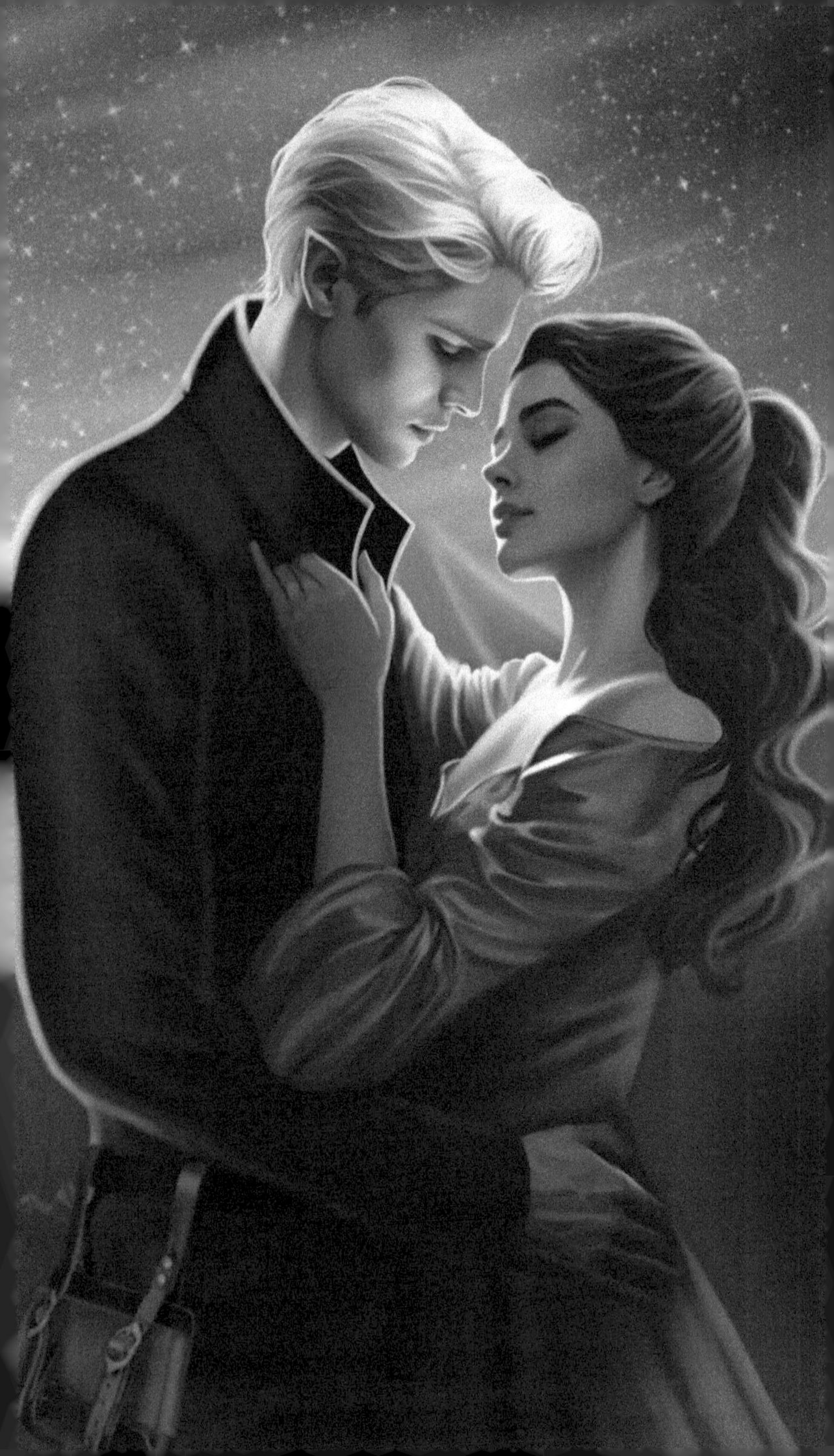

CHAPTER SIX
BRONWYN

The cold air of the mountains whips through my skirts as I hurry through the courtyard back into the second-year building. Sofarynn's office is situated where many of the staff's quarters are located, built into the stone wall that surrounds the academy. They call it the city of stone due to its sheer size.

The main portion of the academy is comprised of three buildings, each as large as castles themselves, one for each year a student spends at the academy. Within these buildings are training halls with special wards to keep deadly spells from tearing down the academy, multiple libraries for quiet studying, and all the classrooms and living quarters for both students and the teachers for that year.

As well as students and professors, the academy also houses the most prominent minds in magic and history, people known as the scholars whose sole duty it is to document and record everything within their field of interest. Their building is situated behind the three houses. There is also a grand chapel dedicated to Meruna, the goddess who created magic, for the more devout of the students to visit.

I was raised by a heretic, and while I do not serve the demigods myself, I do not know what I think of their parents, the gods.

And then there are the rooms built into the grand wall that house the staff, the cooks, the maids, and Sofarynn as well as the others who tend to the library.

I look up, squinting at the high spires of the buildings ahead of me. I catch myself heading toward the first-year building out of habit, but no, I'm a second year now. I've been completely transplanted with the rest of the students of my year. Each year the students move to the next house until they graduate after the third year as full Magickers in their own rights. I sigh slightly at the thought; well, most students will graduate. I'll be long gone with my stolen spellbook and never truly hold that title.

I am so many things, but a true magicker will never be one.

Sure, when I take my role as my father's magic wielder, I'll call myself that but deep down I'll know that I'm no true magicker.

The entry hall is empty as I shoulder open the large double doors. Everyone has probably already made it to their specific classes. I'll be late if I don't hurry. For the most part, classes in the academy are voluntary. Students choose what to focus on and which professors to sit under the tutelage of. Much of the first year was to help get a grasp on basic entry level skills. Common spells such as fireballs and healing and their applications. The different types of enchantments and how not to overstrain yourself applying them. Histories of the great magickers of yore.

For year two, we are given the opportunities to branch off into specialized fields of magic. Want to be a healer? Then you sit under a professor of the healing arts, and it goes on for every variation of magic from combative to passive magic such as enchantments. There's even a class on learning the written variation of magic: runes.

But Petrov Hansimov was known for his control over the waters and waves. He is perhaps the most renowned water magicker, but water magic, while not popular, is also not a lost art. It's taught in this very academy.

And if I am to grasp the complex spells I will find once I get ahold of his spellbook, I will need to have quite the advanced grasp of water magic. Which is why even though I'm not at this academy to earn the title of magicker, and I'm not here studying as an actual student, I have decided to attend this class in particular.

It's part of the excuse I gave my father on why I don't have that spellbook yet. I told him I'm not ready to wield, which is absolutely true. Not that I believe a man as powerful as Elwis the Eel would actually buy that excuse. I doubt he has any idea what it is like to ever feel powerless.

My heeled boots click against the stone as I make my way through the stone halls, finally coming upon the room. I slide in, taking stock of the people in attendance.

I spot Wilder almost immediately; his white hair and pale skin are like a beacon that immediately draws my gaze to him.

Next, I spot the noble lady who has a bodyguard. I'm not entirely sure what her story is, but I saw her around the halls last year. I've heard rumors that she was instrumental in revealing a plot that one of the first-year professors was performing unholy magical experiments on the students.

I had been so focused on avoiding Wilder's torments that I completely missed that.

It was kind of humiliating that something so large could take place completely under my nose.

I twist my ring around on my finger as I force myself to stop dwelling on that.

I spot one or two of the noble blooded friends that Wilder spends time with and then there are a handful of other students, but now that each of the second years are expected to prioritize, I doubt any of the classes will be as full as they were in our first year when we were just trying to soak up as much as possible.

Now we have to be picky.

And not many people will pick water magic.

After all, we live on a peninsula entirely circled by mountains. Very few people here have even seen the coast.

What precipitation we get usually freezes over, and ice magic is a different class altogether.

But still, there are some who are curious enough about water or oddly passionate about it. Perhaps, they grew up admiring Petrov Hansimov and want to excel in the magical field he was known for.

It makes me wonder what classes I would choose to attend if I actually had the liberty of doing so. I'll admit that I am very interested in this water magic. Father always taught me that people will overlook power because of inconvenience, and I feel as if this is an example of that.

Any less well-known field of magic leaves the opportunity of discovering spells overlooked by others, spells that could be the difference between life and death in a magical battle.

The professor, a man I recall is named Morozov, is standing in the center of the room. The desks are arranged on platforms in a half circle around the central podium. The professor is a Lowlander, which is no surprise, as the only human race capable of wielding magic they make up a large part of the magicker population. He has black hair that is swept carefully back at the nape of his neck and wears blue robes so dark that they almost appear black.

However, it is his pallor I find exceptionally striking. He reminds me of Wilder.

Just as I think that the professor looks up, and I catch a glint of red.

I sit up, gripping the edge of my desk. I strive to keep my face impassive even as my thoughts are racing. What does this mean?

Professor Morozov is a vampire as well.

My eyes dart to Wilder, and I shift slightly when I see that he is watching me. Why are there so many vampires in this academy?

And what exactly are they up to?

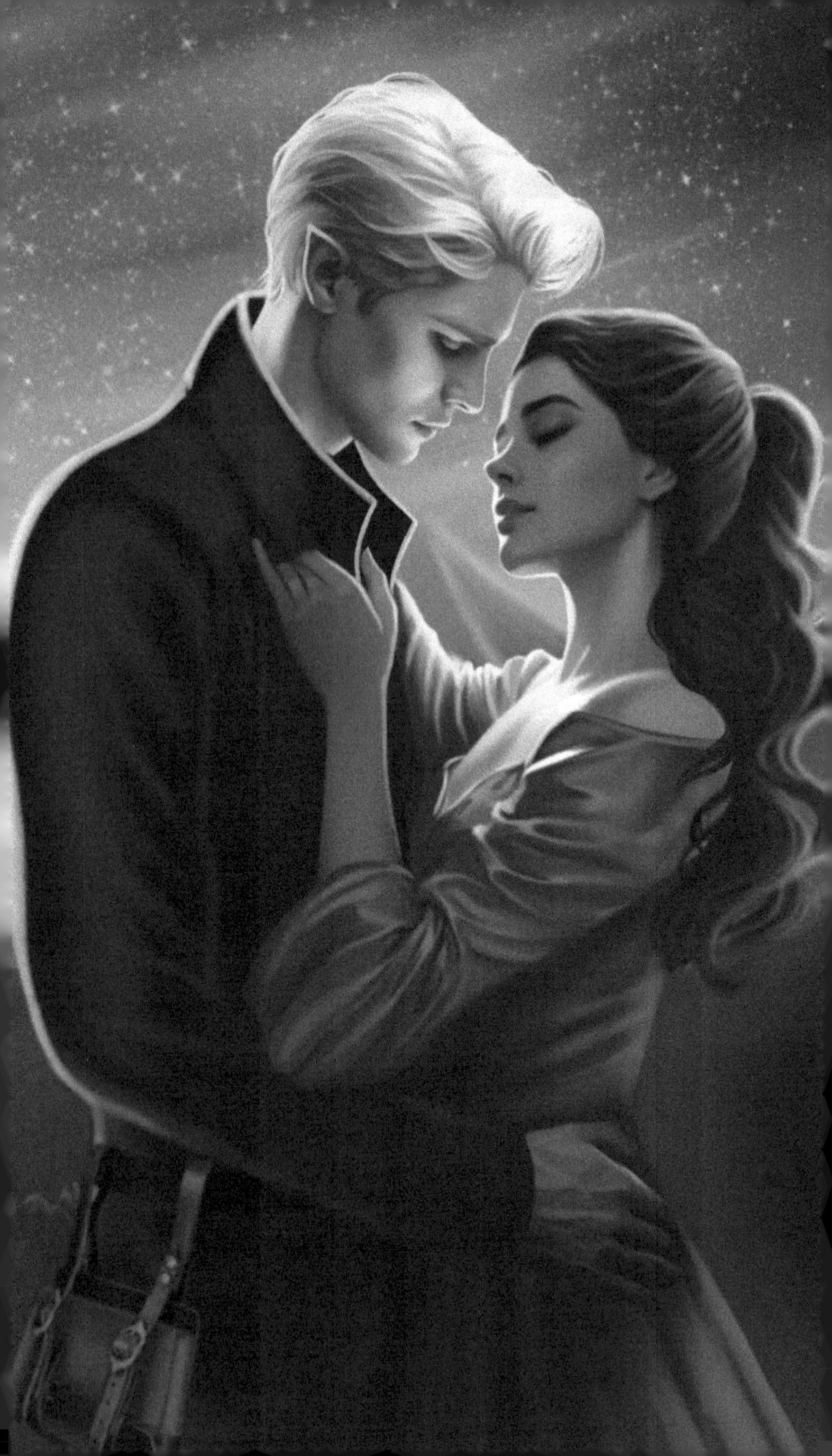

CHAPTER SEVEN
BRONWYN

I will be honest, despite my purpose and who my father is, I never actually expected to find myself breaking into a professor's locked office in the middle of the night.

Breaking and entering is Corallin's territory.

Willfully ignoring the laws in place for her own gain is my twin Natasya's territory.

I like to think that I got Father's rationality. His penchant for seeing the bigger picture and ability to carefully concoct plans based on that.

His shrewdness if you will.

It normally makes me the calculating one, the one who sits back and gets one of my sisters to do my dirty work. I'm the one who pulls the strings and keeps my conscience clean. But I'm here alone and my sisters are far away, and I have always had a weakness for curiosity.

Which is why I find myself fumbling with lockpicks and cursing my clumsy fingers. The pick tumbles to the floor, and I switch to cursing Corallin. If she wasn't so jetting good at lockpicking then maybe I would have taken it up, but as it is there were no locked doors that remained that way for long around my sister. There never arose an opportunity or a necessity for me to learn the skill.

I bend over, running my hand across the stone until my fingers knock into the pick. It goes sliding, but I manage to snatch it up before it gets away.

I sit back on my heels and glare at the door before I jam the lockpick into the hidden pocket of my dress that my mother sewed for me to hide the artful tools of my father's trade.

As I study the door, my hands lower to the spellbook attached to my belt, and I begin flipping through it for a spell that I can use to open the door. If I keep trying to pick that lock, I'll be here all night.

I thumb through the worn pages whispering a quick spell that I already have memorized for illumination. A small glowing orb appears, bobbing next to my shoulder as my eyes move over the pages of my scrawled penmanship.

So much for the stealth that I was trying to attain, but I can't very well read in the dark. I just have to hope that everyone else in this wing of the building are sensible individuals and are now in bed. Well, except for the vampire that I'm trying to learn more about, but I am already taking a gamble with him. I only pray to whichever deity might be paying attention that he isn't here. After all, there is a whole academy for this creature of the night to stalk through, why would he be cooped up in a musty old office?

Besides, no light shines from underneath so unless he is sitting in the dark, I should be in the clear.

And just maybe if I can get into this study, I can learn what he is doing here. And if he was the one who turned Wilder into a vampire. If so, why?

Why would *anyone* want to make someone as vain and conceited as Wilder immortal?

It seems almost like an eternal punishment for humanity to me.

"Aha," I whisper as I finally find a spell that I think will do the trick. It's an ice spell, but just summoning ice won't do what I need it to do unless I intend to freeze the lock and break it. However I'd prefer to keep it, so the good professor doesn't know that I was here.

No, this spell not only summons ice but manipulates it to take a specific mold. It's longer and more complicated than a regular ice spell. I don't remember where I found it but probably in some musty tome and I thought it would be handy, so I jotted it down. This is just another area where one of my sisters would succeed much more easily than me.

Natasya could use her sorcery to manipulate the lock and turn the mechanisms within. Sorcery is capable of changing and manipulating any existing object—even the dead as my father and sister are so fond of using—but magic can only ever create something new.

Still, perhaps this ice key will work. I whisper the spell, making certain to form each syllable carefully. If I say one thing wrong, then the spell could go awry. I could wind up creating a creature of pure magic to fight at my side instead of summoning the ice like I want.

The temperature drops, and my breath fogs in the air in front of me as there is a cracking sound. A light fog appears, condensing before it clears to leave a jagged piece of ice protruding from the keyhole. Hopefully, the rest of the ice filled in the space beyond and is now pressing on each mechanism that needs to be lifted and pressed to work the lock.

I turn the ice piece carefully, moving painstakingly slowly to make certain that I don't snap the piece I'm holding. Cold slices across my skin like tiny daggers, but I grit my teeth and keep at it.

A click sounds, and the doorknob dips slightly. I let out and exhale as I push it open, peering in. As far as I can tell from my vantage point, the room is indeed empty. No vampires lurk within.

I push to my feet, whispering a heat spell that immediately melts the ice key.

I brush off my skirts as I stride into the room, balling my numb fingers into a fist so that they will warm up.

Now, if I were a vampiric professor with a hidden agenda, where would I hide my personal correspondence and other incriminating letters that might just reveal what I'm up to?

There are stacks of papers lying on his desk, but I doubt any of those will reveal any sort of pertinent information. No, the stuff I'm looking for would probably be kept in a hidden compartment. I move across the room, checking behind picture frames and tugging on the spines of the books before I move to the desk. I run my fingers along the edges, looking for loose panels.

I'm so engrossed in my work I don't realize that the door has swung open and that I'm no longer alone until a voice says, "Well, well, well. What have we here? Hello then, Eel. Fancy running into you here."

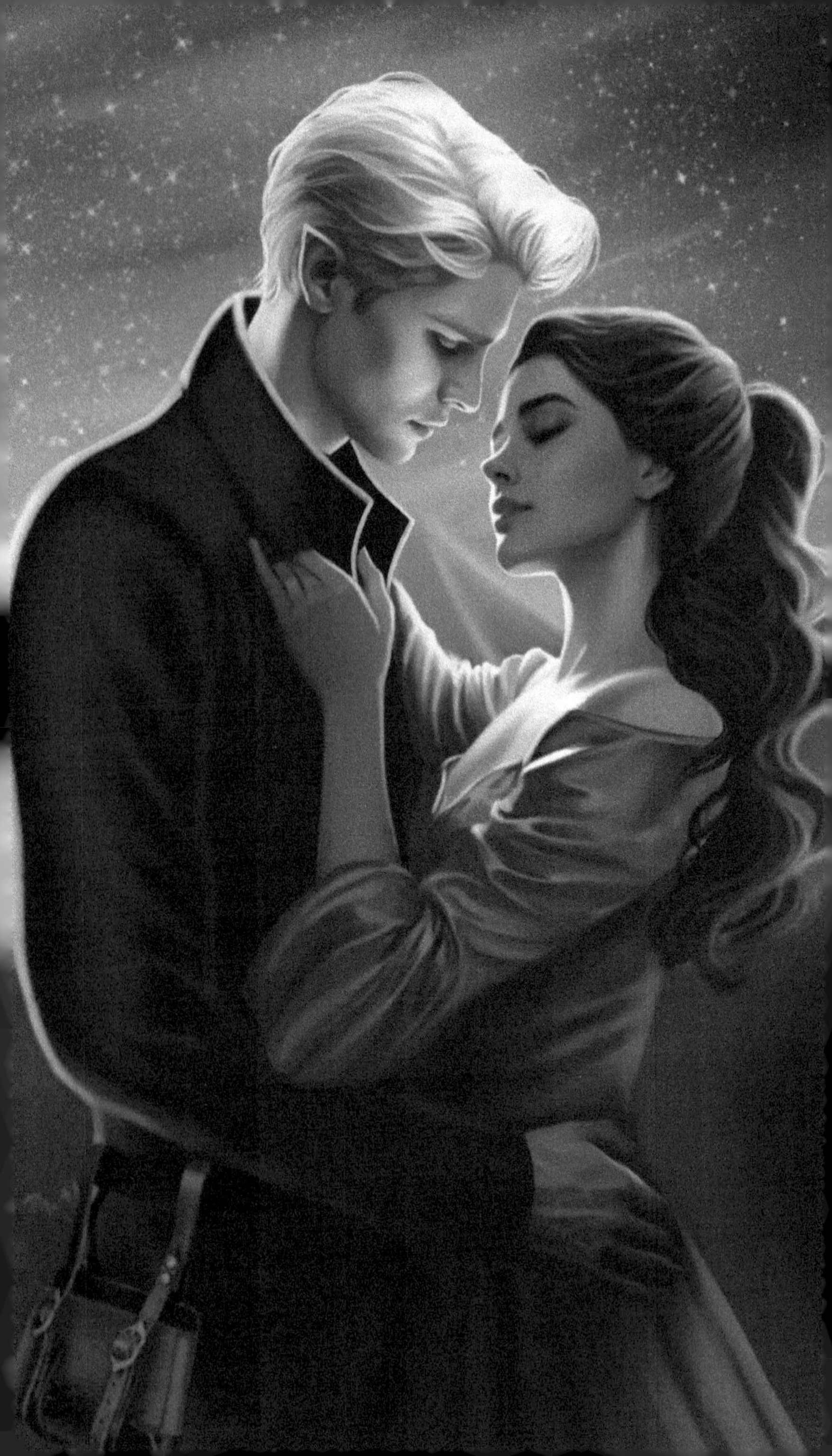

CHAPTER EIGHT
BRONWYN

I gasp, jumping and whipping my head around to see none other than Wilder standing there with his shoulder against the door frame. His white hair practically glows in the poor lighting. He reaches out, running a hand over the water dribbling from the lock, holding it up. The droplet glistens in the bobbing light of my sphere. "But you are just full of surprises."

I straighten so fast that I knock over a stack of papers on the desk. They flutter to the ground, landing in heaps at my feet. My eyes dart to the door that I had relocked behind me then back to Wilder. If anyone was going to walk in on me, he was the last person I was expecting. "How did you get in?"

He smirks, holding up a gleaming brass object. A key. "I asked nicely." He drops the key, catching it midair and arches a single pale brow. "But this isn't about me. What are you doing in here?"

"I... uh," my mind races for an explanation, until I realize that I don't owe him one. "I don't need to tell you." I bend over behind the desk and begin picking up the papers just as much to hide my expression as to clean up the evidence of my presence here.

"Oh, I think you do. That is unless you want the good professor to know of your nightly visit." His voice is dripping with moral superiority when in truth he doesn't have a moral leg to stand on. Any morality he may have once had is a rotten hollow husk that was eaten by his ego and cruelty.

"And risk revealing that you were in here as well? I think not." I keep my attention on the papers as I try to show him just how little I care, but then something catches my eye. It's my name written across the parchment.

Bronwyn the Eel. Father Elwis the Eel is a notable merchant and landowner. Mother Vala owns a reasonably successful inn. She and her two sisters are all adopted, original parentage unknown—suspected a low-class farmer. Seems reasonably proficient in magic and a quick learner but lacks ambition. Is the first magic wielder in her family line. What can she offer? Money but not much else.

I reach out, spreading the paper revealing the sheets underneath it. There are more names. Meruna Kotov, Asimov... name after name. These sheets are filled with the names and information of the students here at this academy.

"Difference is, my dear Eel, that I was asked by the good professor to come to his office, and I'm willing to bet that you were not so get explaining before I grow bored." There's a moment of silence and then he heaves a frustrated sigh. "Are you even listening to me?"

I push to my feet holding the paper with my name on it. I turn it toward him. "What is this?"

Wilder goes still, and I look down to see that there are two or three papers of a similar parchment held in his hand. I squint back down at the paper and gasp. "This is your handwriting!"

Wilder pales even though I had not thought it possible for his pallor to increase, but it seems I was mistaken.

I step around the desk, clenching my jaw. "Wilder Zubkov, why is my name on this paper? Why is my father's name on this paper?" I shake it in his face. "Just *what* are you up to?"

His eyes dart to the paper clutched in my hand then back up to my face. A tinge of red, just the faintest hue of color, meets his cheeks. "N—nothing."

I don't know what is more unsettling, that Wilder had all this information about me, that he would dare accuse me of lacking ambition, or that now professor Morozov has this information about me.

And why would Wilder think I lack ambition? He is the one who is riding on his daddy's powerful name while I'm here actually making a name for myself and not relying solely on my father's influence.

I stalk toward him, crumpling the offending paper between my fingers. "This certainly doesn't seem like nothing."

Nervousness flashes across his face before it becomes as still as stone.

"Does this have anything to do with the fact that you're a vampire?"

He flashes his teeth, I'm not sure if it's a smirk or a grimace, but it's enough to reveal the pointed edges. They could be mistaken for simply sharp teeth to the untrained eye, but I was raised by a vampire, and I know what a fang looks like.

My eye is very trained, and it is focused on Wilder Zubkov.

"Is this really what you want to do, Eel? Do you really intend to extort me when you're the one who broke in here?" He lowers his voice, leaning toward me. His fingers glance across my arm, cold as ice, at least I presume that it was because of his touch that a shudder runs down my spine. His hands stop at my hand, prying my fingers from the paper and taking it back. "And what made you think you could threaten a vampire in a dark room all alone in the middle of the night?"

I snort, yanking away and folding my arms. "If you think I should be afraid of you, you have another thing coming at you." My eyes flick up and down him, from the tips of his polished shoes to his white hair. "Cause no matter how scary you try to make yourself out to be, I know the truth. You're nothing more than a common pest."

"That's a funny way to address a monster of the night."

I step toward him, raising my chin as if daring him to make good on his threats. My neck is exposed. I notice his eyes dart down to it, and he swallows, but there is no bloodlust in his eyes. Instead, that nervousness is back.

Good.

"My father is the stuff of nightmares," I whisper. "Compared to him you are a gnat."

As soon as the words are out of my mouth, I regret them. No matter how far Wilder has gone, or what he has done to humiliate me, I've never invoked my father. It's important that people only ever see him as a powerful and influential merchant. A businessman. A counselor and friend to some of the most powerful people of Ruskhazar.

But never anything more.

They can't know that he runs a criminal empire, that he is a necromancer, or that he is a vampire. All are things that are highly frowned upon in polite society.

Confusion dances across Wilder's features, but just then I hear footsteps sound outside the door. There is a growl and a, "Where is that boy?"

I feel my eyes widen as they fly to the door. I can already see a shadow moving into it. It's too late to try to hide. I look up at Wilder half expecting him to be smirking at my trapped state, but he looks just terrified.

"What?" I begin in a low tone, but I'm cut off when he lunges forward, slamming his lips against mine.

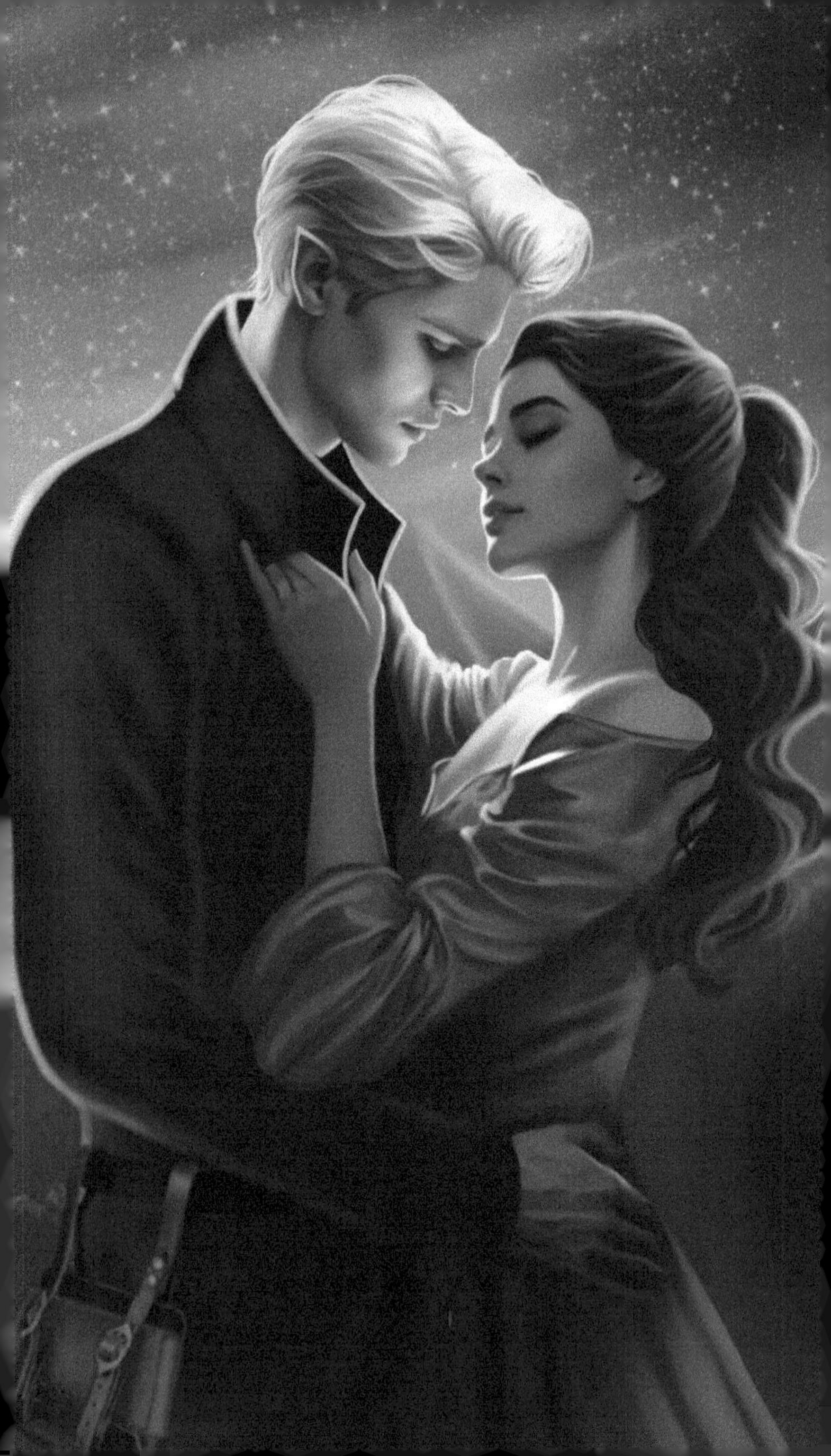

CHAPTER NINE
WILDER

A part of me is screaming that I've gone absolutely insane, especially as Bronwyn begins to struggle to pull away, and I am forced to circle my arms around her to keep her in place.

What would possess me to put my lips on the Eel girl? If my father is to be believed and you can become tainted by association, then I am very, very tainted by this merchant's daughter.

Panic. Pure and simple. This is what I will blame this on. I heard Morozov coming, and I panicked. I am unsure why my panicked response is to kiss Bronwyn, but that's something that I will have to dwell on later.

I simply knew that if the professor caught her in his office without a good excuse, then he would end her. And as annoying a creature as she may be, I don't necessarily want to see her ended.

And so, I kissed her. *Gods*, I kissed Bronwyn the Eel, what is wrong with me?

"What in Skyhold's name are you doing, *boy*?"

I pull away, feeling oddly lightheaded, something I attribute to the disgust I'm sure I'm currently experiencing. It isn't helped by Bronwyn immediately shoving me away. I reach out, grasping her hands to keep from losing my balance.

I drop her hands immediately, but she is still looking at me. Unmitigated murder flashes in her eyes.

Dear gods, forget about the vampire in the doorway. This woman is going to kill me.

"Wilder," she gasps out, her tone seething with rage. I take a small step away from her for my own safety.

I whirl, praying that she doesn't say anything further to ruin my plans. If she gives away that we are not lovers stealing a moment in a darkened room, then I will have kissed her in vain.

"Don't worry, dearest," I say past clenched teeth. I hope that my words convince him that I love this girl because my tone leaves much to be desired. "I shall handle this." I turn to Morozov, holding my hands out in a pacifying gesture. "Professor, I—"

"Not another word from you, Zubkov. I gave you my key to access my office when I'm not around. Not so that you can…" he trails off the disgust apparent in his tone. "Who is this girl anyway?"

"She's uh…" I trail off as I glance at her, my mind suddenly going blank as I take her in. Her hair is disheveled—did I do that?— and her eyes furious, and all around she's truly breathtaking. My mind is sluggish and filled with unhelpful thoughts about how beautiful she is right now and wondering if she kissed me back, that I can barely remember just what I'm saying and why. "This is Bronwyn," I finish dumbly.

"Is she a candidate?" Morozov demands, never one to be distracted from his plans of creating a vampire population.

However, his words have the same effect as dousing me in freezing water, reminding me of the direness of this situation. And just how close he can come to killing her. The Eel girl may be trouble, unfortunately distracting, and just a little frustrating, but I certainly wouldn't want her to become the next of Morozov's victims.

He has not remained a vampire in the academy this long without spilling more blood than he can even consume. "Certainly not," I reply with a snort.

"Hmmph, I'll be the judge of that." He eyes her up and down. "Tell me, girl, of your talents."

"None," I say hurriedly stepping in front of her, hopefully breaking Morozov's contact with her. I tilt my head slightly. "She's a bit dull and couldn't cast a spell to save her life."

I hear Bronwyn gasp loudly behind me, but don't turn around. I can't afford to have my thoughts scrambled by looking at her again. I need to have my wits about me.

"Why are you associating with such a useless creature then?" Morozov asks, arching his brow.

"I happen to like useless creatures," I state defensively.

"I suppose that like calls to like," the professor says glibly. I fight the urge to wince. He takes a step to the side, and I mirror his actions keeping myself between him and Bronwyn. She must seem to sense the danger because she keeps her mouth shut, proving me wrong about her being dim at least. "But we have a special job for useless things." His tongue snakes out, licking his lips as a hunger enters his eyes.

Oh gods, why won't he just give up and let us leave?

"So does my father," I blurt out.

This causes Morozov to pause. He may have no respect for me, but my father is another story.

"I'm to marry Bronwyn." I can barely believe the words coming out of my mouth. I don't know where this story is coming from because it certainly wasn't my brain. My tongue just decided that it had a life of its own and started wagging. "She may not be much, but her father is quite influential."

At this, Bronwyn smacks my arm, quite hard. I hope Morozov takes it as a sign of affection.

"Hmmm," Morozov says slightly taken aback. "Your father did not mention any betrothal."

I slowly slide my hand into my tunic's pocket. I'm still holding the paper with Bronwyn's information on it. I can't have it going and proving me a liar by proving that her father is only a merchant. Albeit an influential one, but not nearly someone so important that my father would ever consider having his only son wed this merchant's daughter.

"And why would he tell you? It isn't as if he needs your permission on what to do with his own son."

I'm lying so much that I'm surprised that Dagmy the goddess of lies doesn't materialize in front of me to congratulate me for digging such a massive pit for myself with my words.

But this finally gets Morozov to snap his mouth shut.

"Now if you will excuse me, I was in the middle of something before you interrupted us." I reach back, snagging Bronwyn's hand and yanking her toward the door after me.

Blessedly enough, the professor lets us leave. I breathe a sigh of relief as we clear the room, but that sigh is proven to have been premature as Bronwyn yanks me to a halt in the hallway and hisses, "Wilder Zubkov, you have two minutes to explain yourself before I kill you."

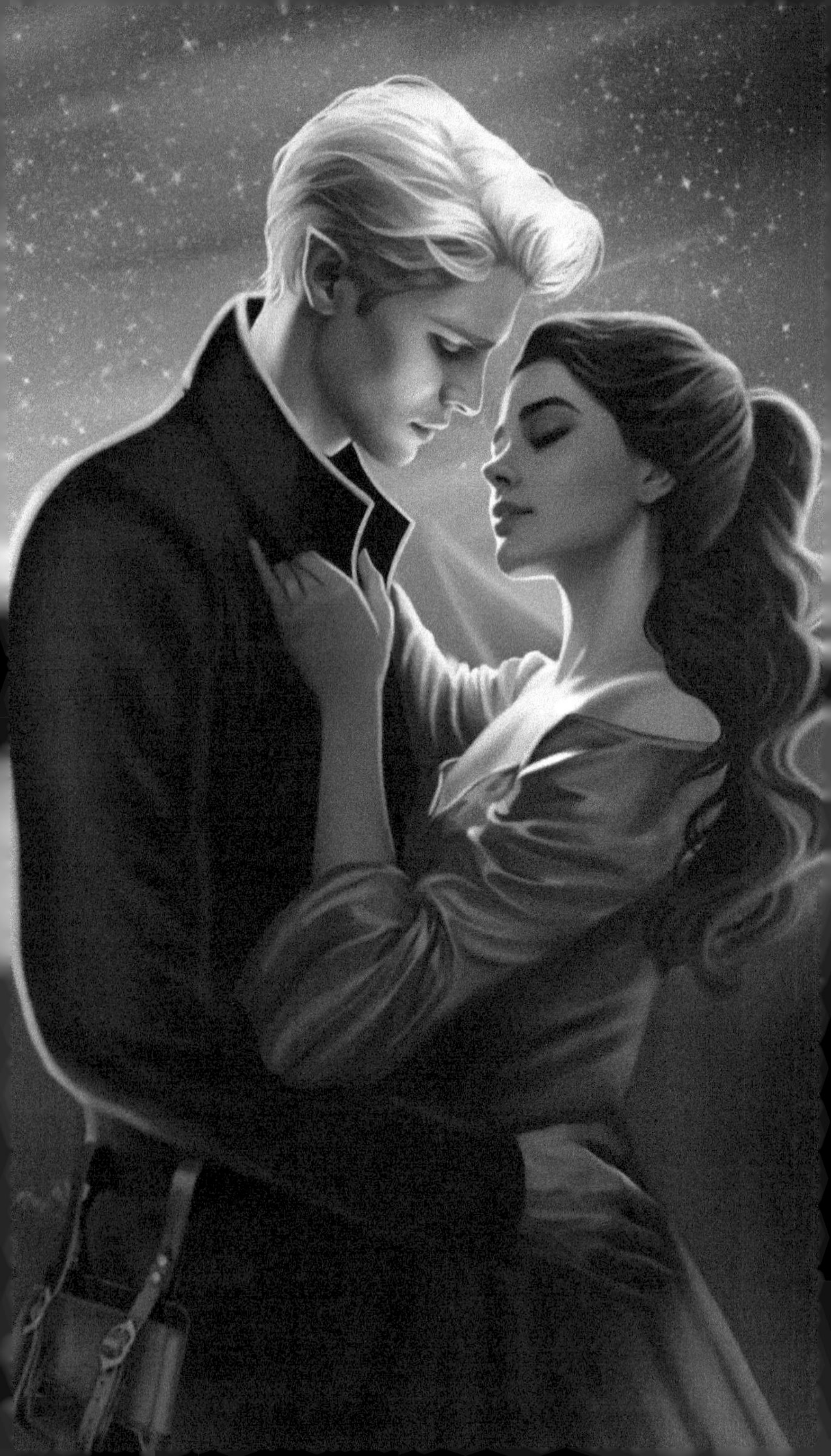

CHAPTER TEN
BRONWYN

My father taught me how to kill my man. I have several techniques up my sleeves. Ways of killing them quickly, drawing it out, or doing it in a way that it appears to have been an accident.

This specific skill set is not one that I have ever felt the need to use. Indeed, I have often prayed against it ever coming to such drastic measures.

Until now.

Wilder's eyes dart down the empty hall before he exhales. "Not here. We should talk somewhere private."

While most students have to sleep in common rooms for their genders, the academy does offer the luxury of private rooms to those with the money to afford it. Naturally, I have one, I'm sure that Wilder does too. But I'd be hanged if I brought Wilder to my room, and I'd be twice hanged before I went to his room.

"I know of a place," I finally reply reluctantly. It's a place I've gone for isolation, at least in the first-year building. I assume the second building will have one as well.

It's the roof of the towers of the building. They are usually left alone. Not many want to put up with that many stairs and with multiple towers even if one is in use—usually by overly affectionate couples—then I can always go to a different tower.

I turn on my heel, striding down the hall. I check over my shoulder twice to make certain that Wilder is still following me, but he doesn't make a run for it. Which either proves that he is braver than I had originally thought him to be, or he has no idea the Skyhold I'm going to give him.

He kissed me.

How *dare* he?

Honestly, he is lucky my father is nowhere nearby or else that would have been the last thing he ever did. I have half the mind to make it the last thing he ever does.

But I've always been the most rational of the Eels, and the most reluctant to resort to bloodshed. I'll hear Wilder out and decide whether to push him over the edge afterwards.

Wilder, for his part, is quiet as I lead him up the winding staircase to the top of the tower. I find the platform beyond empty, although I'm not sure who else would be mad enough to be out this late at night.

I step through, inhaling the cool night air deeply. The platform is only a few paces across on either side, but from up here, I have a view of the whole valley around us. In the distance, the mountains' shadows rise up like dark bruises on the horizon. Above, the stars twinkle down, never allowing the night to be too dark.

I turn, bracing my hands on the stone wall behind me as I take in Wilder.

"This should work," Wilder says, peering down the stairs before he shuts the door. He leans up against it, exhaling slightly. "There are eyes and ears everywhere inside the academy."

I wonder just who he is worried will hear us. Is this about his reputation, I mean Skyhold above forbid he be caught kissing an ambitionless merchant's daughter, or is there something else going on?

"You owe me answers," I say curtly.

"You owed me answers first," he replies smoothly, crossing his arms. He arches his brow. "Or did you forget that you had *broken* into a professor's room. I caught you. The only reason you even got away with it is because I..." he pauses sneering. "I covered for you. You owe me, Eel."

"The only thing I owe you is a bloodying of that pretty straight nose of yours."

He reaches up, touching his nose with a frown. "You're such an ungrateful, miserable thing. I suppose I can't blame you though, it's just the result of your poor breeding."

"My breeding is just fine," I say straightening. "At least I have enough tact not to kiss people who despise me. What sort of a pathetic attempt was that, Wilder?"

He snorts. "The only thing I was attempting was to save your life. To insinuate anything else would just show the depths of your ignorance, and how delusional you could be. As if I'd ever *willingly* choose to kiss the likes of you."

"And what was I in danger of? Dying of the boredom of your company?" While I certainly could have gotten in trouble for rummaging through the professor's office, it isn't as if he could have done anything about it. He is a professor; there are strict rules against harming students here at this academy. Vampire or no.

Although, there are always certain men who ignore such rules. My father being foremost on the list.

Still, even my father would not choose to kill if it would bring repercussions unless he had no other recourse. Unless he felt threatened.

Perhaps by someone learning something that he would have rather remained a secret...

Maybe this professor has a larger end goal than just tutoring us on the mechanics of water magic. And Widler is right in the middle of it.

Of course, it's so simple I don't know why I didn't place it before, but I will place much of the blame on Wilder's kiss which seems to have done a number to scramble my brains.

I pull back, tilting my head. "Does this have anything to do with you now being a vampire?"

Wilder's throat bobs, telling me that I'm at least partially correct. But all he says is, "I am not saying anything unless you tell me what you were doing in Morozov's office."

"Fine," I say reaching up to rest my finger on my chin, my other hand grips my elbow, hard. My attempt to keep my cool composure. I hope that it works and that on the outside I look entirely unbothered even though my mind is racing with questions and theories. "Let's make a deal. We both want answers for the other, so I will answer your questions if you answer mine."

He raises a brow, the white hair glowing in the starlight. "A question for a question?"

"A question for a question, and don't even think about lying to me, Wilder. I'm very good at figuring out people's tells."

"Likewise, Eel."

I swallow hard when I realize that he is actually agreeing to this. A part of me wants to walk away. None of this is actually important to my grander purpose here. The vampires, Wilder, even the paper with my name on it—none of these things actually matter in the long run. I am here for a spellbook and nothing else.

If anything, this game of sharing secrets will reveal too much and threaten what I'm actually supposed to be doing.

And yet... my curiosity will not allow me to continue onward. Not without knowing, not without figuring out what is happening.

There is something foul afoot here at this academy, and it involves the undead.

And Wilder might just be my best bet at figuring out what it is. Which is how, despite my better judgement, I find myself arching my brow and smirking slightly. "So, who should go first?"

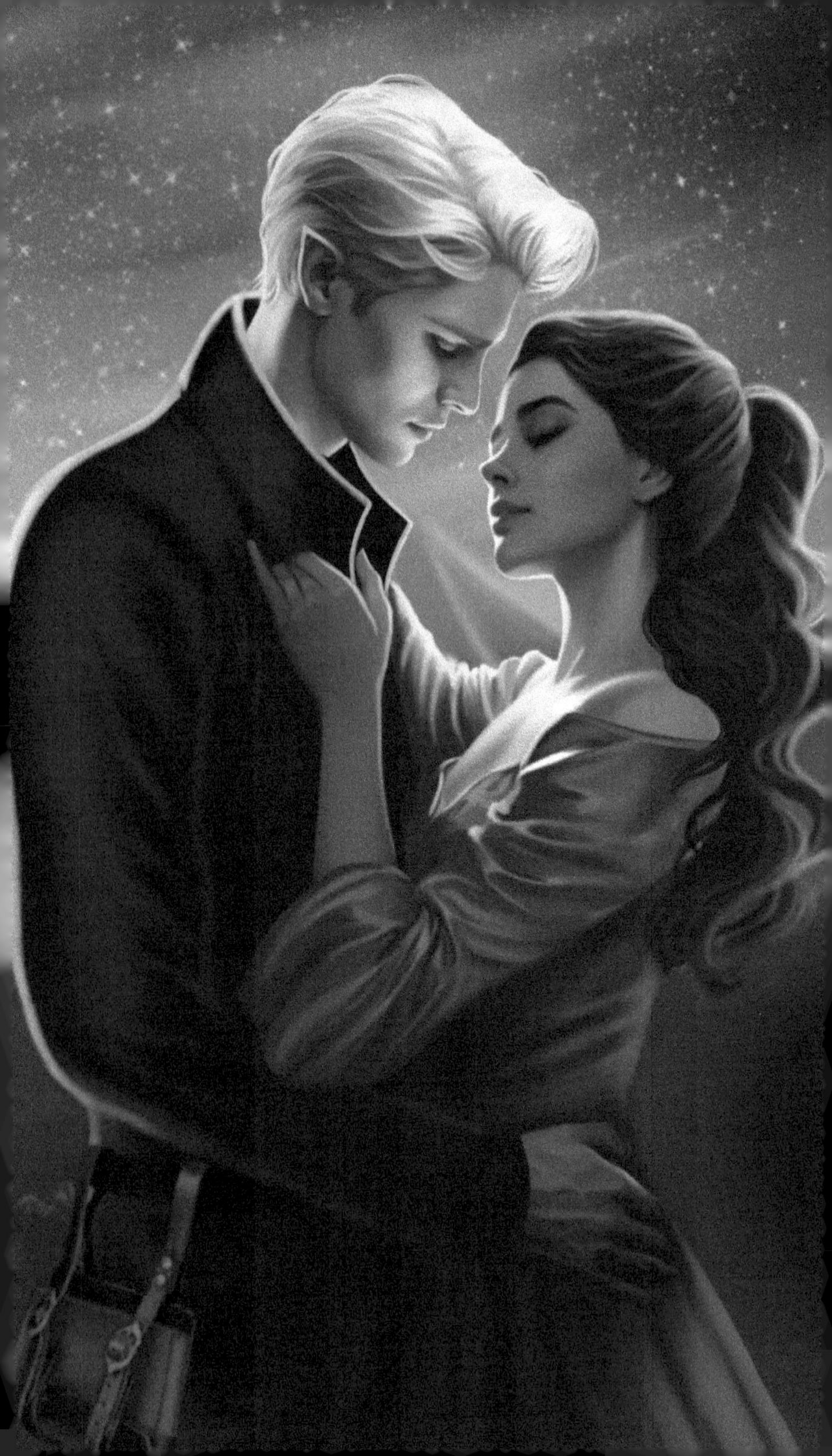

CHAPTER ELEVEN
WILDER

Despite my better judgement, I find myself playing along to Bronwyn's insipid little game. And all on the grounds of accursed curiosity.

I should walk away, wash my hands of her. If she wants to get herself killed by picking a fight with a bloodthirsty vampire, then that is her problem.

I have my own issues, a host of them. If there were droplets of water, I would drown in them. I do not have time for this girl, and her windblown brown hair, and her problems.

I should turn around and stride right back down those stairs, but I don't. Instead, I find myself adjusting my cuffs and watching her. "If you are going to jetting suggest that the gentlemanly thing to do is allow you to ask your questions first then I will remind you that I am no gentleman."

"You don't need to remind me," she grumbles. I wonder if she is thinking of the toad in her bed, my parting gift to her last year. I had thought it would be the perfect final prank because then it could go on to eat any remaining bugs I had put in her room that she had failed to catch.

I smile slightly at the memory. Ah, what a time that was, back when I was at the luxury of being cruel and my whole life wasn't inverted on itself.

I had always thought highly of myself then, never stopped to consider my actions or wonder who I was. That all changed when my father made me a monster.

Maybe I always was one, after all, I shared blood with one. But it was easier to pretend then.

"But you kissed me, so..."

I let out a frustrated breath. "If I offer to be the first to be interrogated, will you stop bringing up the kissing?" The sooner she does the sooner I can get my mind to stop replaying it over and over through my memories.

"Not remotely," she says with a small smile. "It's my destiny to never allow you to live that down. When I draw my last breath, it will be to recount that moment."

I groan.

"But I will offer a temporary respite from it if you tell me *why* you kissed me."

"I didn't do it from any desire to do so if that's what you're accusing me. It was simply the only way that I could think to save your life in so little time and with you affording me so little opportunity."

She snaps her mouth shut. It's dark, but I swear I can almost make out that quizzical gleam in her eyes. She takes a small step toward me. "How would that have saved my life?"

I hold up my finger with a smirk. "Ah, it's not your turn to ask a question, now, is it?"

She glowers but says nothing. "What were you doing in the professor's chambers when I caught you?"

"Trying to find a secret compartment in his desk. Now, tell me what you meant when you said you were saving my life. What was I in danger of?"

"That was hardly an answer," I growl when I realize that she is looking at me expecting me to tell her.

"You asked, I answered. Are we going to keep going?"

I exhale slowly. "I was worried how the professor would react if he caught you going through his belongings."

"How did you think he would react?"

I hold up a finger. "You're terrible at this. You just can't ever stop talking, can you?" Bronwyn looks like she might hit me, so I take a small step back as I mull over my thoughts trying to sort through the questions I'd like to ask. I need to settle on one, but with so many burning questions it is hard to pick just one. "What were you hoping to find in Morozov's office?"

"Answers."

I fold my arms over my chest as I step closer to her so I can glare down my "straight pretty nose" at her. "You can't be that vague, that's a violation of our agreement. How would you like it if I just started giving you one-word answers?"

"You'd have to learn how to get to the point to do that," she says glibly, but then she exhales. "I was suspicious of the professor. With first you showing up as a vampire and then him being here also clearly a child of Neltruna well…" she narrows her eyes as she looks me over. "What are you two up to?"

I let out a nervous chuckle. For all her annoyances, she is sharp. She cut straight to the matter far faster than I had anticipated. I had no idea she had already pieced together so much, like the fact that I'm working with Morozov; although thinking back I see that we left plenty of evidence. It seems as if she has the whole story, and yet, I still know nothing.

It leaves me feeling vulnerable.

"If you already know so much then I don't know why you bother asking me."

"Answer the question," she says stepping toward me, her eyes hold a challenge, but I notice her fingers nervously twisting the ring that she is wearing.

I turn toward the door. "I think I'm done playing this game."

Her hand reaches out snagging mine. She tugs on it, turning me around so quickly that I feel dizzy. "This isn't a game. You said yourself that my life is in danger if Morozov suspects me of snooping. What exactly did I stumble upon?"

I swallow hard. A plot that will forever alter the world... and not necessarily for the better.

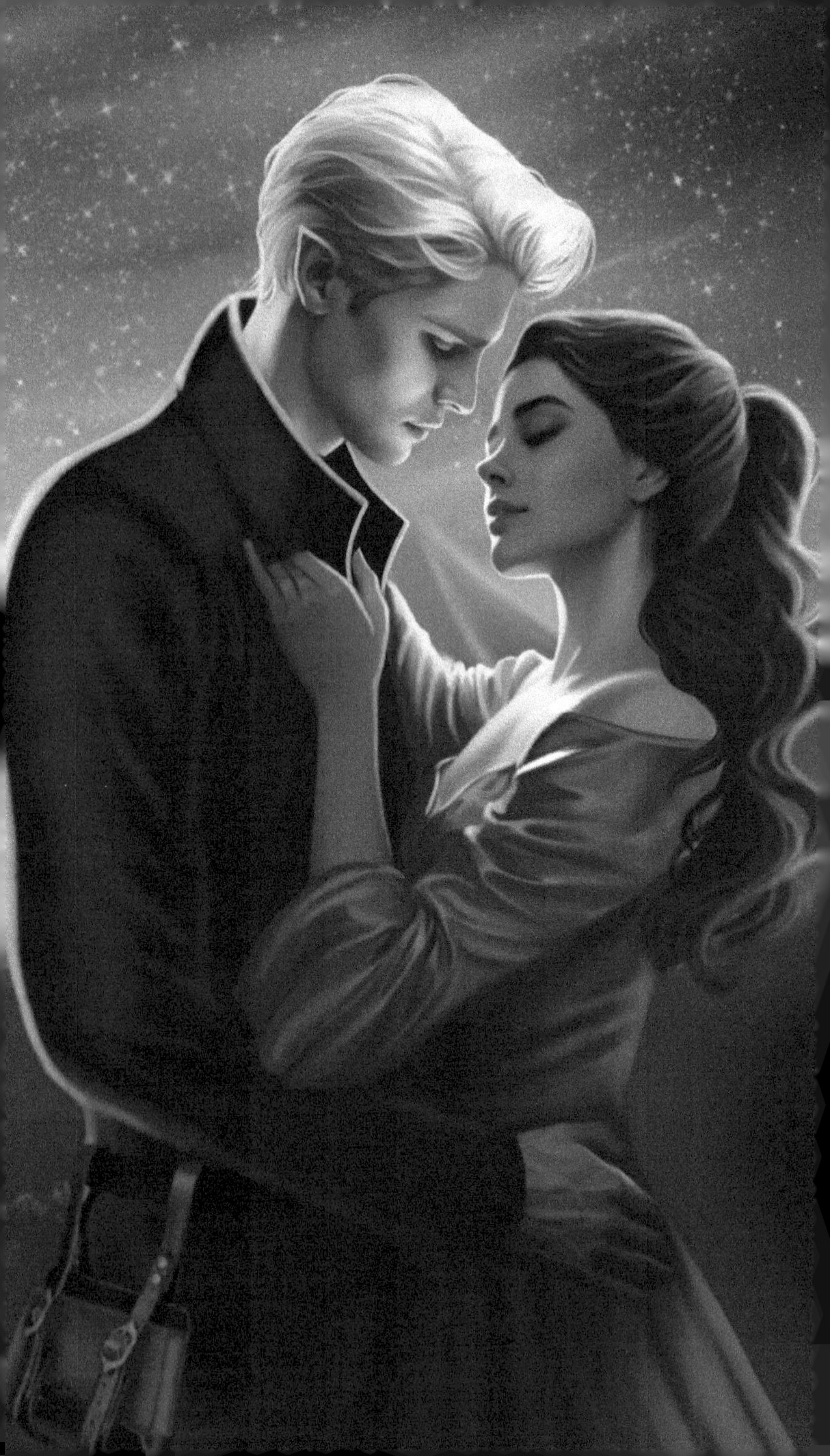

CHAPTER TWELVE
BRONWYN

Wilder is scared. I can read it in the stiffness of his shoulders, the hesitancy in his voice, the way that his fingers tighten just a bit around mine. The Wilder I knew last year was cruel, devastatingly handsome, and suave. Never scared. What does someone like him have to be afraid of?

I look up, allowing myself to stare for the first time into his face. In the dark his eyes just look black, disguising the deep red, but his skin is so pale it practically glows white, like the freshly fallen snow.

I reach up, slowly hesitantly. I'm not entirely sure what I'm doing until I'm resting the palm of my hand against his cheek. "What did they do to you?" I whisper. His skin is cold under my touch, as I'm actually touching the snow.

"They made me a monster," he whispers, his tone breaking a bit on the last word.

"Do you mean to tell me that *this* was not what you wanted?"

He snorts, breaking the spell between us, pulling back. I release my breath, dropping my hand and also moving away only just now realizing how close I had been standing to him. I'd been practically standing atop his shoes.

Wilder releases an exhale that the cold makes visible in the air between us, reaching up to run his hand through his silvery hair. "Why would you think I'd choose to be a vampire? To be among the cursed race? To be an outcast?"

I feel my eyebrow rise slowly. I suppose that I can now guess which of the varied origin stories for vampirism that Wilder believes.

Some say that vampires were created by Neltruna, the goddess of monsters. The first vampires were followers of her daughter the demigod Lady Night, that much most people can agree on. But how they became vampires is wildly disputed. Some, like Wilder here, believe that Neltruna in a fit of jealous rage cursed her daughter's followers to become monsters since they worshiped Night instead of the goddess of darkness herself. Others believe that Lady Night gifted her followers with this form of immortality, her own way of trying to usurp her mother and create monsters of her own.

That's the belief my father always held.

And then there are those that would consider vampirism a disease, given that it can be spread from person to person, but I put no stock in those theories.

How could a disease cause eternal life?

No, it is either a blessing or a curse, and perhaps I am too optimistic, but I like to think of it as a blessing. It helps to make the thought of my future of an eternity as a vampire easier to live with. But as I look upon Wilder, I see all my fears and reservations staring back at me.

Father has always said that someday we will all become vampires, he cannot, nor will he, live in a world without us so we must become as immortal as he is. But he left the timing of it up to us. Corallin was already a vampire when she was adopted, but Natasya and I have been waiting.

Waiting for what, I'm not entirely sure. Until we're older? Until we feel a little more ready?

I am not eager for this fate, but I'd hate how I'd feel if I was left with no choice at all.

"Who made you a vampire?" I ask at last.

"I don't think that it is your turn to ask a question," he replies, morphing before my eyes back into the arrogant boy I always knew him to be.

I roll my eyes. I'm not entirely sure if that is the case, but I lost track, and it is getting too late to argue. "Fine then. Ask your question and then answer mine."

"Why are you not afraid of me?" he demands. "Most people would turn against me if they knew what I was but you..."

I shrug slightly. "I'm not afraid to become a vampire, I don't think you'd attack me, and even if you did, you couldn't kill me even if you tried for a thousand years."

He guffaws and I roll my eyes. "Now are you going to answer my question?"

All humor dies off Wilder's face. "This was... my father's doing. He has *plans*." I open my mouth to ask, but he cuts me off by holding his hand up "I will not delve into that. You are in enough trouble with what you know and now Morozov thinks that we are a couple."

"And whose doing was that exactly?" I ask, planting my hands on my hips.

Wilder groans as he paces away, walking to the edge of the balcony and leaning out over it. "Morozov is a dangerous man, Eel, you should not be taking this matter so lightly. If he finds out that we lied..."

"So, we make certain that he doesn't find out."

He turns toward me, his sneer evident in the moonlight. "We despise each other, it isn't exactly as if we will pass for lovers."

I find myself nodding. "You're right—"

"Oh, gods help us, that's exactly what we need to do," Wilder says with a groan throwing back his head. "We have to be in love."

"*What?*"

"He will kill you if we don't at least look the part, and there's no knowing what he will do to me if he finds out I lied to him." He shakes his head, holding his hand up. "That's it, we need to pretend to be engaged."

"For how long?" I choke out. How long exactly does he think that we can keep this up, because this conversation is perhaps the most civil we have ever been to each other and even this is a strain on civility.

"As long as it takes for me to figure out what to do," he says, jabbing a finger in my face. "And I'll hear no arguments from you. After all, I'm the one attempting to save your life."

I jut my chin out. I hope he isn't expecting me to declare my undying gratitude over it. "You just won't say from what. Only that Morozov is dangerous."

"He is not the sort of man you double cross, I can tell you that much. He isn't the type of man you want to cross paths with at all."

I exhale a breath moving back a few steps as I lean on the wall. "And how exactly do you expect to convince *anyone* that we're engaged, let alone keep the ruse up?"

Wilder reaches up, rubbing at the back of his neck as he looks at me. "Oh, I will do my part to sell the lie, never you worry. The question is, Eel, how good are you at pretending?"

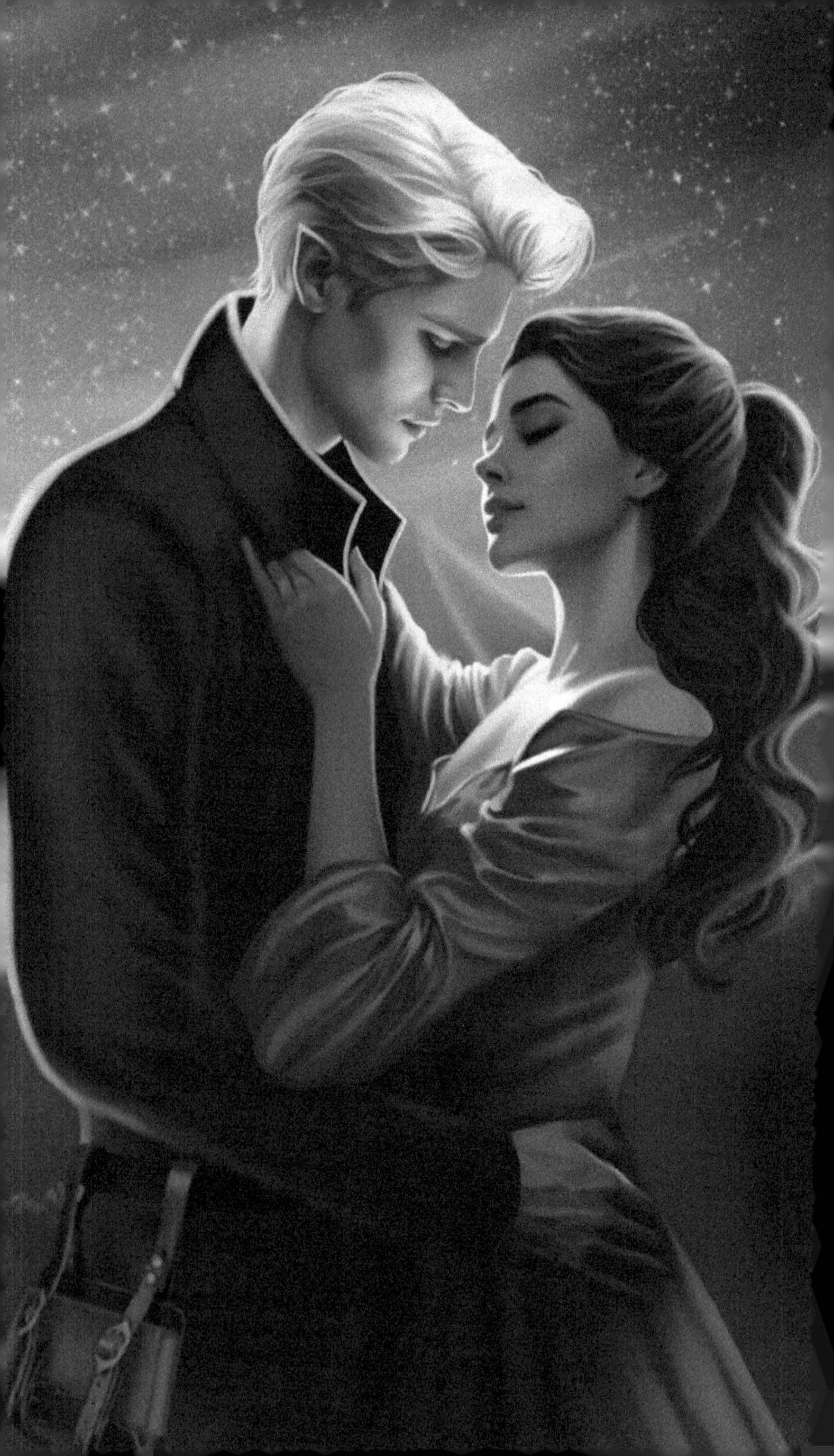

CHAPTER THIRTEEN
WILDER

I feel like I'm coming away from our little tryst with more questions than answers and only a half-baked plan on what to do with the problem that is Bronwyn.

But I also know with utmost certainty that if I had stayed there much longer that I would have spilled my heart to her. And I don't even want to think of what I would have done if she had caressed my face again.

I would have made an utter fool of myself, past the point of any conceivable redemption, and all for a girl named Eel.

I find myself shuddering as I race down the stairs.

"Wait!" I hear Bronwyn call at the top of the stairs. "Wilder!"

I ignore her, of course, it's perhaps the only sane thing I've done this evening.

I told her what I came to tell: that Morozov is a deadly foe, and she must do what she can to remain outside his notice, if such a thing is still a possibility for her after what transpired tonight. I told her that she would have to convince him that we are indeed engaged, and that I would do my part in that convincing.

Naturally, I had wanted answers as to what Bronwyn was doing in the professor's office or how she knows what she does about vampires, but I long ago learned that I can't always get what I want.

There is more to Bronwyn than what first meets the eye; she is an enigma wrapped in a secret and locked away in a mystery. I'm not sure how I could have ever thought that she was a mere merchant's daughter. She is far too cunning for that.

No, she is... something *else*. I'm not quite sure what, but *something*.

And I'm beginning to wonder at her intentions for being in the academy. Something tells me that just learning about magic is something beneath a girl like Bronwyn. She wouldn't be here unless the academy had more to offer, but what is that?

A husband? She never talks to anyone.

The status of a magicker? Not likely.

It must be something and I'm just missing it.

I give my head a sharp shake. I can't afford to be distracted from my own ulterior motives by wondering about Bronwyn's. I'll keep her from getting killed but that is all she shall get from me.

I have enough problems of my own to bother with the beguiling Bronwyn the Eel and all her mysteries.

No, the real question is whether Morozov is expecting me to come back so he can fill my head with more plans for a world domination I don't even want.

I slide my hand into my pocket, my fingers meeting a piece of paper that crinkles under my touch. I feel my mouth quirk up as I pull the paper out and see Bronwyn's name. That smile slides off my face as I read over my scathing summary, I wrote for her.

Did I really say that she lacked ambition? Only to now be thinking that she is too ambitious for the simple life of a magicker and is currently at this academy with nefarious intents?

And Bronwyn read this?

I crumple the paper back up in my hands. I know that I had been cruel on purpose; Morozov has tasked me with writing reports on my fellow students so that he can know who to pick for the vampire army he is growing.

I'd done it to save Bronwyn, because no matter how annoying she can be I never wanted her to be involved. And yet despite my best attempt, she wound up getting involved anyway. Which makes my effort to make her look bad completely useless, which would be bad enough except she had to go and read my failed attempt.

Now, she probably hates me for hating her, when in fact out of all the students at this academy, she was the one I was trying to protect.

Even if Morozov turned everyone here, I had been determined to save one. Bronwyn. In saving her, perhaps I might have been able to save myself.

But now, that whole plan is in flames. I'm still undead, there's a power mad vampire intent on creating an army like him out of the students here, and the one person I specifically tried to save went and got his especial attention.

To top it all off, now I have to pretend to be madly in love with Bronwyn the Eel, a feat that will require all if my lying skills because I feel more inclined to strangle her for getting me into this mess than to show her any sign of affection.

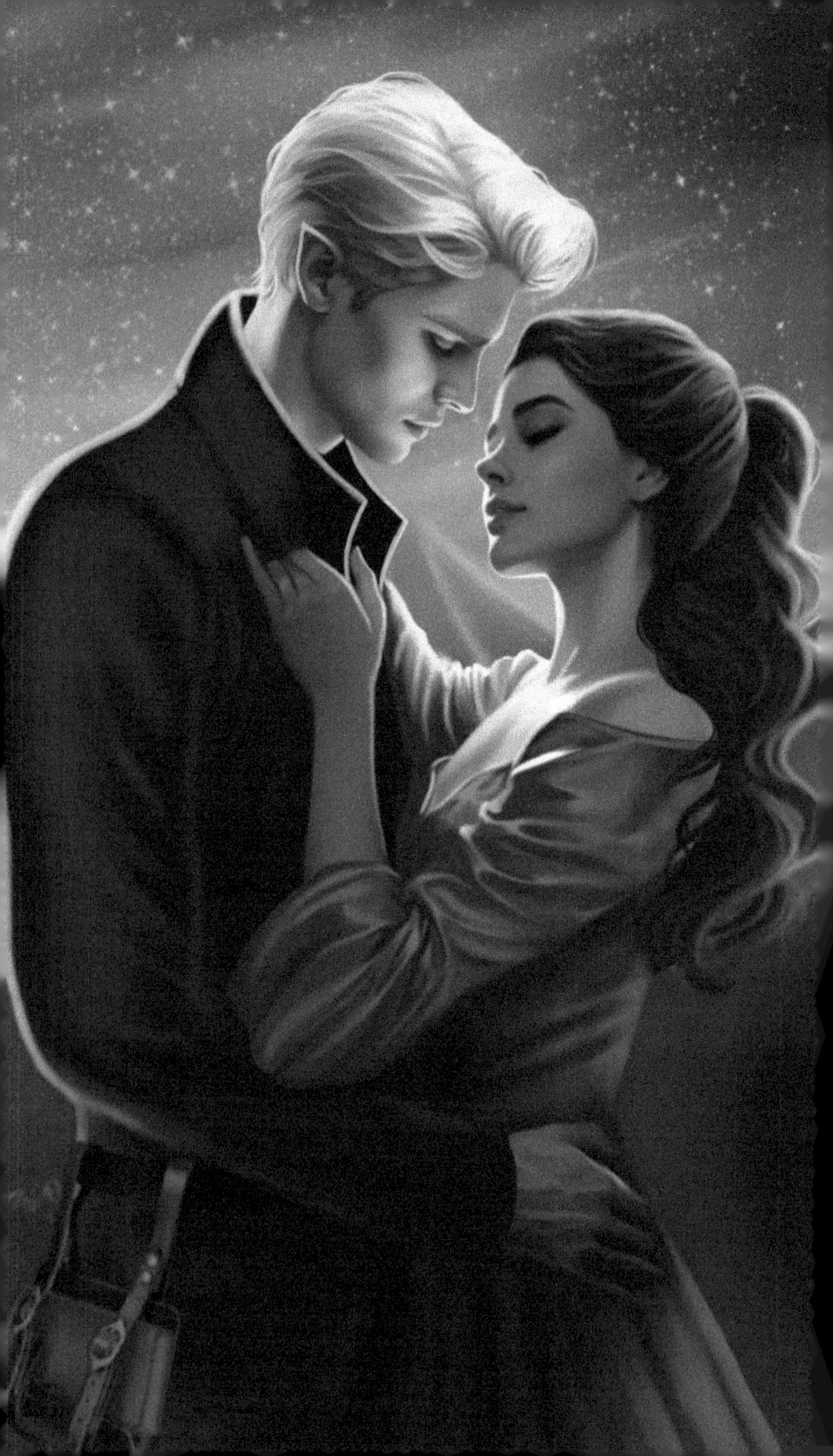

CHAPTER FOURTEEN
BRONWYN

It has been a strange past few days, even for me. And I was raised by a secretive crime lord and a comely innkeeper alongside my twin and our vampiric adopted sister.

My life has never been normal by any stretch of the imagination, but I think that kissing Wilder is perhaps the most surprising thing that I have ever experienced.

And I walked in on my father murdering one of his business associates when I was eight.

I hate that out of everything that transpired last night—from discovering that both Wilder and Professor Morozov are in league to the half answers I pried from Wilder later—the one thing my mind keeps straying back to is that kiss.

It was nothing, it meant nothing, it explains nothing.

If I want to know what is going on I should focus on the connection between Wilder and Morozov and how they both became vampires, not keep reliving that kiss in my mind.

Over and over, without ceasing, without respite, remembering how it felt, wondering if I kissed him back.

It's disgusting, really.

My thoughts shouldn't be on Wilder at all, mystery or not. I have a spellbook to steal. A sudden influx of vampires in the academy is not my concern.

"Oh, Miss Bronwyn, how fortuitous. I was hoping to see you."

I halt dead in my tracks. I'm at the entrance hall of the second-year building, my lunch in my hand on my way to Sofarynn. The corridor ahead is streaming with sunlight as it filters through the high arched windows, but there standing in a dark alcove just outside the front hall is Professor Morozov.

There is nothing fortuitous about this. The professor was lying in wait for me. Which means that he has taken enough notice of me to know where I take my afternoon meal.

"I don't know how much Wilder has told you..." his tone carries a threat. It's very clear that he is checking to see what I know, and if he doesn't like the answer... well, *I* probably won't like what happens next.

Wilder's warning rings through my mind. He had said that Morozov was a threat. I'd at first laughed it off, the academy has strict rules over what can be done to students, stricter now after last year. Even if Morozov is a vampire, I have nothing to fear from him. Surely, he doesn't feed off the students.

But then I start to wonder if that's actually true. If a psychotic professor could kidnap students to carry out his sick experiments on them then who is to say that Morozov is not also operating under the academy's nose.

"Nothing that his father doesn't approve," I reply with a smile that I hope passes for sweet and innocent and that not too much time passed while I was considering my response. If Wilder is scared enough of this man to pretend to be in love with me then perhaps, I should be just a little frightened of what such a man is capable of.

"And what might that be?"

I force a small giggle. It sounds insipid but hopefully not strained like how I feel. "Oh, you know the usual. Sweet nothings and promises of a future."

Morozov's eyes narrow further, and I feel my smile slip slightly. He doesn't seem to be buying my naïve act. It's all I can do to keep my eyes from darting to his mouth and the deadly fangs hidden within.

I've seen firsthand how quickly a vampire can strike.

"Just who is your father again?"

"Uh..." I begin, but I'm cut off as someone grabs my arm from behind. I jump until I hear Wilder say.

"Bronwyn, my darling, there you are."

I try not to stiffen as Wilder drapes his arm over my shoulder. I tell myself that it is only because I can feel the coldness emanating from his skin, even through his clothes, that a shudder runs down my spine and my breath catches.

"Professor," Wilder says with a small nod. "I'm surprised to see you here." His tone carries a hard edge of accusation.

"I was just having some words with your lovely fiancé," the professor replies. "Making certain that we understand each other."

"Good luck with that, I'm afraid that there is very little she understands."

This time I cannot stop myself from stomping on his foot. Besides, my skirts hide the movement.

"It's a good thing that she has a pretty face and a lot of coins," Wilder says his voice coming out breathy with the pain. His smile is plastered across his face. "Otherwise, I could have been paired with someone too smart for her own good and with an ugly face to boot."

"I'm just still so surprised that your father thought now was an appropriate time to begin considering the holy nuptials," Morozov mutters, his tone heavy with accusation. "Especially with all our... *plans*."

It's all I can do to keep my face blank, to try to sell the illusion of the brainless fiancé that Wilder is creating.

Wilder waves his hand as if trying to swat the words from the air before they reach him. "My father is nothing if not capable of multiple schemes at once. My dear sir, did you think you were the only person he was conspiring with? How silly of you, he never gives anything his full attention. I should know, I'm his son." Despite Wilder's flippant tone, I can sense the deep hurt buried underneath his carefree façade.

Morozov's eyes dart to me but I quickly turn to Wilder, mustering my most sympathetic look as I reach up, trailing a hand across his cheek as if I'm trying to console him. I suppose there is a part of me that does pity him. I don't know much about Wilder's relationship with his father, but I can see in his eyes whenever he mentions him that it is not a good one.

I could have been so easily like him if not for Elwis the Eel adopting me and showing me unconditional love. I can only shudder to imagine what sort of person I would be if

I had not been rescued from my abusive birth father. The few memories I have of him are nightmarish.

If I had been left in his care, I would have become just as cruel as Wilder, if not more so. After all, it is our fathers who show us who we are. Elwis showed me that I was a priceless treasure to be cherished.

My birth father showed me I was worthless, not even worth coming home to some nights, or making certain that Natasya and I were properly fed.

What sort of person did Wilder's father teach him that he was?

I lean toward him, resting my head against his shoulder, twining my arms around his arm. I give him a slight squeeze, and he stiffens. I squeeze him again, this time in warning.

Morozov frowns as he watches us.

"If you have a problem with this, then I suggest you take it up with my father," Wilder states. "But I think you will find you've overestimated your place in his esteem. He is not one to take kindly to questioning of his methods."

Morozov looks like he wants to argue further, but Wilder suddenly stiffens. "Come on, Bronny," he states, whirling. I loosen my grip on his arm, and as my hand slides down, he snags it, pulling me along behind him.

He sets a punishing pace, clearly wanting to leave this conversation as quickly as possible. I glance over my shoulder at Morozov, still standing there in the shadows as we head back deeper into the building.

I release his hand as soon as we round the corner. Wilder flexes his fingers, probably trying to remove the feel of my hand pressed against his. I know that my fingers tingle as if I'd been holding snow. "Never call me Bronny again," I say stiffly.

He nods, his nose wrinkling with disgust. "Agreed, Eel." He turns, looking over his shoulder. Probably to ascertain that the professor isn't following us. "That was an uncomfortable conversation." His jaw twitches as he turns back to me. "What is it going to take for him to stop being so suspicious?"

"It seems that whatever you are up to... it's very big. It has the professor quite on edge."

Wilder swallows, averting his gaze.

I release a sigh. "I had actually intended to eat outside."

"It's too sunny." Wilder shudders. "I cannot join you."

"I didn't intend for you to join me."

"And how would you explain that to the professor if you turned around and went outside without me after we just did our level best to convince him that we are happily engaged? He probably thinks we're off to sneak an embrace or do something equally disgusting."

I release a sigh, my shoulders slumping as I glance down at the bundle of food wrapped in a cloth and tied to my belt next to my spellbook. I suppose the world wouldn't end if I didn't eat with Sofarynn for one day.

"How long is this scheme of yours and Morozov's going to take? When can we go back to normal?"

Wilder's features darken as if a shadow has visibly crossed his face. "There's never going to be a normal again if my father and Morozov have their way."

I tilt my head as I study his features, trying to determine what caused that sudden mood shift. "And you? What would happen if you get your way?"

He releases a long sigh. "If I want to live a life without being hunted as a monster then I have no choice... my way is the same as theirs."

I give my head a shake. "You're a mystery, Wilder Zubkov."

"You're one to talk," he mutters. "You're no mere schoolgirl. I know that much."

I feel myself smile. "We already have a relationship founded on a lie. Naturally, there would be some secrets to crop up."

Wilder exhales. We walk in silence for a long moment before he grasps my arm. I pause, stiffening, but his hands are eerily gentle as he turns me toward him. His eyes, though red, are earnest as they look into mine. "I know that you don't trust me, but I just want you to know that I would never let anything happen to you."

"Never say never," I reply, fingering my spellbook's belt and the frayed ends of the cloth. "The world is a dangerous place."

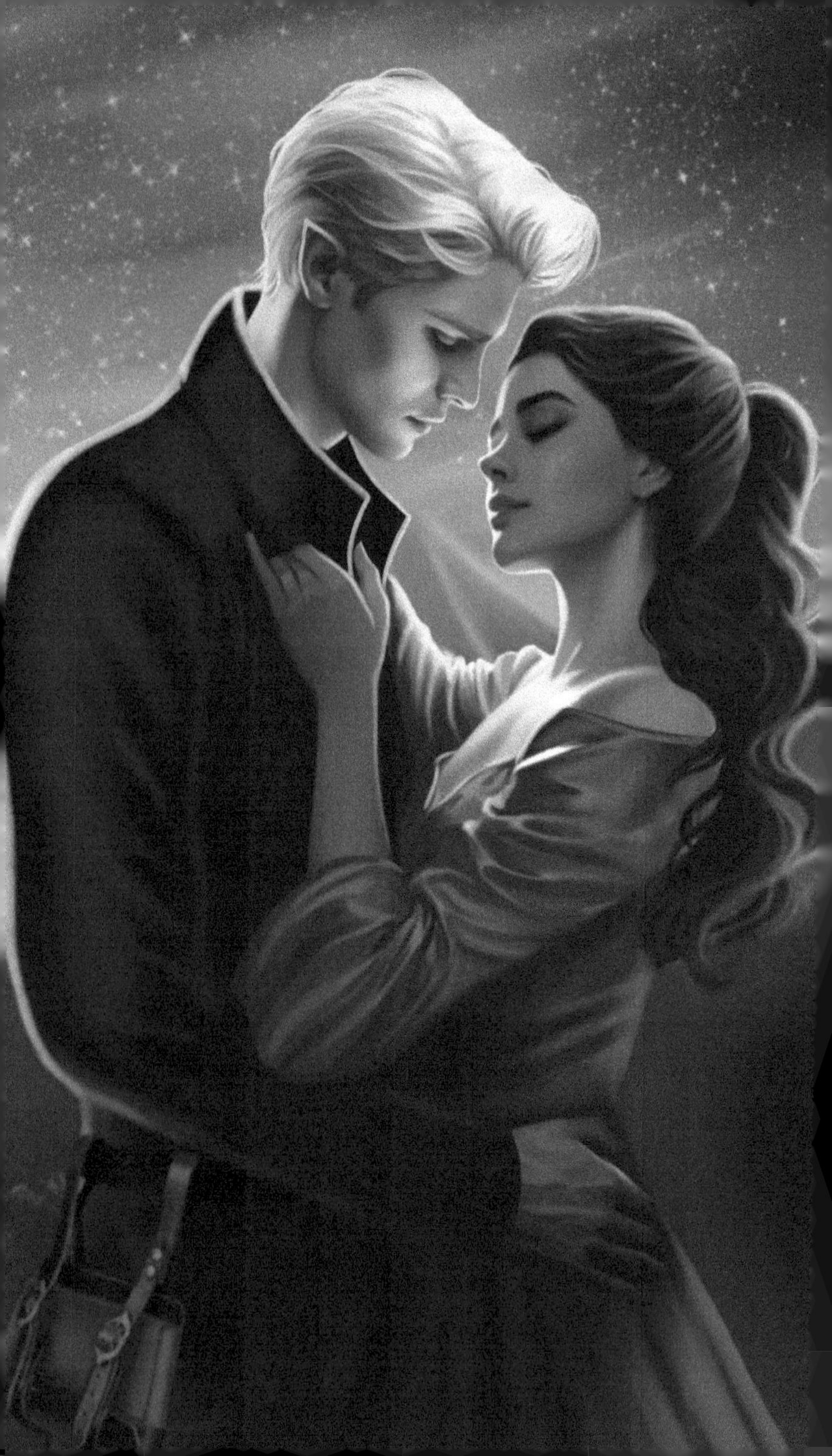

CHAPTER FIFTEEN
WILDER

I don't know if I am being paranoid, but it seems as if Bronwyn is avoiding me. Well, perhaps not avoiding me, but she is focused on her daily tasks of attending her classes, studying in whichever library I happen to not be in, and eating her lunch with some caretaker.

She acts as if we are not currently in a fake relationship.

How can I convince Morozov that I'm madly in love with her if she and I are never around each other?

I glance down at my drink, swirling the red liquid in my chalice. My friends think that it is wine. I like to pretend that it is wine because the truth is far more gruesome.

It's blood. I brought vials of the loathsome liquid with me, taken from slaughtered livestock, because I cannot go more than a few days without sating my thirst.

My father said that I would be gaining great power when he made me become a vampire. When in reality all I got from it was an addiction.

I hate this part of me so much that the only way I can choke down the vile substance is by pouring it into a glass and turning it into a social event. I will talk with my friends and try to fool myself into not paying attention as I take a few sips.

Try to pretend that I'm drinking wine the same as the rest of them.

I grimace and tilt my cup to my lips, forcing down a swallow. It slides down my throat, sweet as honey with an almost fruity flavoring. I think the worst part is that it actually tastes wonderful.

"Where is Gregos?" I ask as I lean back, resting my hip against my desk. We are currently in my room, a spacious area with plenty of room to throw a little soiree in privacy as I spend time with my closest fellows.

Not that I can stand Asimov and Gregos, but they are the only people here who are actually my peers. Sure, there are plenty of wealthy individuals and there are plenty of students skilled in magic.

But these two are the only ones with all the right breeding and talent. They hale from both wealthy families and ones that have a long line of powerful magic wielders. They are my equals.

Well, other than a few Lower elf students, but they consider it beneath their notice to associate with *humans*. And they certainly wouldn't be caught dead near me given my mixed heritage. I'm part Higher Elf, and there is enough bad blood between the two elven races to fill this whole valley and drown us all.

So, whether I can stand them or not Asimov and Gregos are the only friends I'm permitted to have.

"Would you believe it, he is sick," Asimov replies with a snide sneer. "Maybe this will teach him to not turn up his nose at the healing charms class I'm taking."

I snort. "That's unlikely. You're assuming Gregos is capable of learning, which I believe the prerequisite for him to do that is to have a brain."

Asimov raises his glass giving me that point before he takes a gulp of his drink. Actual wine. I watch him my stomach twisting in knots of envy as I raise my own glass to my lips.

"Also, you would never believe the rumor I heard some of the students saying," Asimov continues, completely oblivious to my moral turmoil. "They said that you were engaged to Bronwyn the Eel." He laughs as he rests his glass on the mantel before he waves his arm at me. "Don't worry, I told them that I'd incinerate them from the inside out if I heard anyone else spreading that disgusting rumor."

I'm not entirely sure how the rumor could have spread. It was supposed to be between Bronwyn, Morozov, and me.

I didn't tell anyone. I'm sure Bronwyn didn't. Which means that either someone saw us walking while holding hands that one time or... Morozov has been asking some students about it because he still hasn't completely bought our story.

I take a sip of my glass to hide my expression, but the blood goes sour against my tongue. For a second, I consider how to respond to that. Here in the safety of my own rooms, I'm tempted to set the record straight. Especially to one of my only friends, despise him as I may. But I can't risk this getting back to Morozov. If Bronwyn and I are to be in a fake relationship, then I must go the whole way. Including admitting it to my peers.

"Actually, that is more than a rumor. It is indeed a fact," I reply.

"What?" Asimov chokes on the swallow he started to take. His wine goes flying all over him but he only stares at me in disbelief. "Surely you jest."

"I'm afraid not. My father arranged it."

Asimov pulls out a handkerchief and begins dabbing at the wine stain on his tunic. "What could have possessed him to do that?"

"It turns out that her father is quite a wealthy merchant. Influential too."

"You're his only son; surely, he could find a better match for you. There are plenty of wealthy influential people out there. *Nobles*."

"Nobles don't control shipping routes."

"Since when has your father been interested in shipping?"

That's a fair question. Asimov has met my father; he knows what sort of man he is. I can't just give him a half-baked excuse; I need to actually make it sound like him. "There is too much new money," I say, quoting something I've actually heard him say. He feels very strongly on this topic, it's his favorite thing to rage about when he has had a little too much to drink. "Too many no accounts are out there making their fortunes, and those who have had money for generations are no longer the wealthiest. That leaves a power imbalance, one that if left unchecked will render family names like ours worthless."

I draw in a deep breath and shrug. "And so, my father decided that if he cannot defeat them then he must join them. So, ours would be a joining of old money and new." That is not actually something my father would ever say, but I'm hoping that mixed in with direct quotes from him it will be enough to convince Asimov.

Asimov shakes his head with a sigh. "Well, he had one thing right. This will render your family name worthless. First, your father having an illegitimate child with a serving maid. Now, you are marrying a merchant's daughter with no noble heritage? Doesn't he realize your bloodline is already diluted without him adding Bronwyn the Eel into the mix?"

"I'd kindly ask you not to bring my mother into the mix," I reply coldly. I don't care that she is a servant girl, she was the only decent parent I had, and she loved me even though I was fathered by a monster.

"Of course, what a friend I am," Asimov says with a shake of his head. "Here I am stating everything wrong with this when you already know that. I should be consoling you instead." He exhales loudly before he takes a gulp. "I may need another glass for this though. I'm jetting awful at consoling."

"It's fine—" I begin, but he cuts me off.

"It most certainly is not fine. Tell me truly, how are you holding up?"

I open my mouth to reply but whatever I was about to say dies on an exhale. I reach up rubbing the back of my neck. "Not as bad as I thought it would be..." I admit. As far as fake relationships go, this is the best one I've been in.

Not that it is saying much. But there's a part of me that almost wishes it wasn't all a lie. What would it be like if I married Bronwyn?

Frustrating.

But also amusing.

Thrilling?

Yes, that's a word for how she makes me feel.

"What do you mean?" Asimov demands his face twisting in disgust.

"She's not half bad at kissing."

Asimov gags at this, and I feel my eyebrows rise as he rests his hand on the mantel and makes a grand and hopefully forced display of his disgust. "Please don't make a mess on my floors."

I hope he doesn't pay too much attention to my floor. There's a bloodstain from where I spilled a vial that I haven't managed to get up.

"You've kissed the Eel?" he demands.

I shrug.

"Why?"

"I was... curious. Really, I don't see why you're making such a big deal about this."

"You despise her," Asimov counters. "She is disgustingly beneath you."

While it's true that I used to despise her, I wonder how much of that stemmed from true feelings of hate and which were from wanting to get her to notice me. I roll my tongue in my mouth as I consider that.

Gods, that's an unsettling thought.

I quickly shutter it and determine to never think of it again. Because that would force me to admit that I always felt this strange draw to Bronwyn the Eel. Even when she was an insufferable first year with no friends save for the dozens of books she buried herself under. It's fine if I'm intrigued by her now, she is intriguing and clever and a mysterious enigma.

But the Bronwyn I knew last year was not deserving of that interest and the Wilder of last year was an entirely not monstrous person, and he was above needing to be interested in her. That Wilder had prospects, pride, ambition. He wasn't forced to resort to drinking blood and pretending that it is wine.

I reach up, running my hand down my face. "You're right," I mutter in surprise. "I can't believe I *kissed* her."

Asimov shakes his head slowly, his disbelief clearly written across his face. "Let's hope her father is very wealthy to make this pain of yours worth it."

I hold up my glass as if a toast, but I find myself wondering what sort of man Bronwyn's father is. I know who my father is, but I presume that not every man who is unlucky enough to father a child is as powerful, ambitious, and egotistical as him. Some of them have to be decent, right?

Maybe Bronwyn's father is one of those rare ones. It makes me wonder what meeting her family would be like… if we were actually engaged, that is.

The thought is honestly too much to handle, and it leaves me wondering why I even entertained the notion even for a second. I toss back my glass, draining the rest of it in one gulp and resolutely remind myself that *this* is my future.

Not the one I saw with Bronwyn.

The one spent choking down blood and plotting to make more like me.

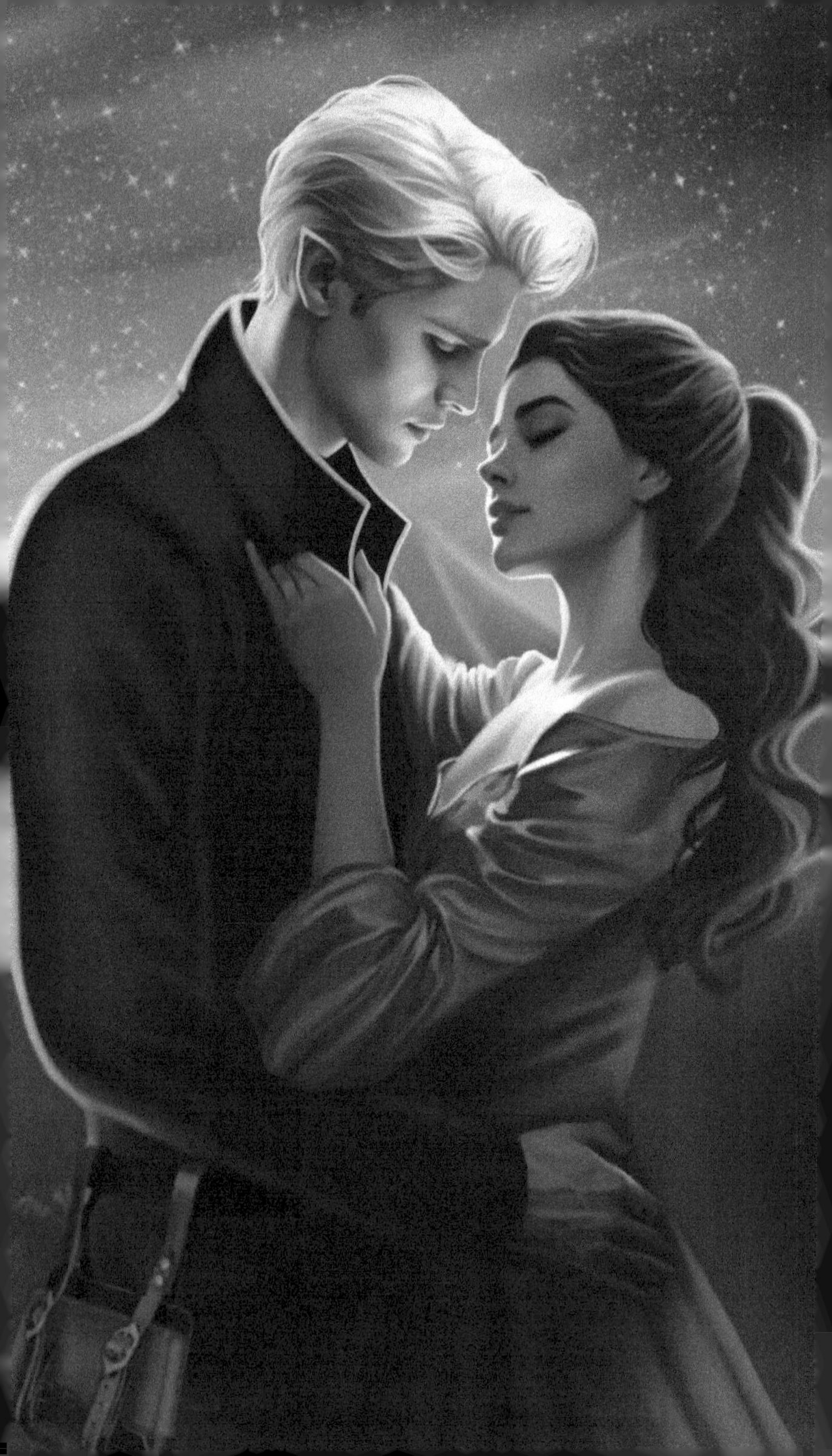

CHAPTER SIXTEEN
BRONWYN

"I was engaged to be married once."

I look up surprised as I take in the large stack of books on Sofarynn's desk and the bookkeeper sitting behind them, her eyes dark and far away. The large chunk of bread in my mouth keeps me from asking what she means, but as she continues, I realize she wasn't waiting for my response anyway.

She seems to be lost in a different time. A different life.

"To a blacksmith, if you can believe it." The corners of her lips turn up in wistful memory. "He was the first person here to show us kindness—my brother and me—when we first came up from the deserts oh so long ago. He opened his house to us even though we were complete strangers. I didn't stand a chance; I fell hard for his heart."

"He sounds lovely," I say finally swallowing my bite.

"He was raising his daughter's son as his own. There wasn't a soul he wouldn't help. I felt like the luckiest girl in the world when he asked for my hand."

"What happened to him?" I ask, a little scared of the answer. It's clear that Sofarynn and this blacksmith did not work out.

"He died," she states flatly. "I killed him in my ambition to discover a new magic. A powerful magic. One that I never had any right wielding." She shakes her head bitterly.

I feel myself stiffen. Does she know about my ambitions? Is this a warning to back away from trying to get that spellbook?

"What are you getting at?" I demand, resting my hand on my chair. My head is screaming at me that I should run.

"I've heard of your relationship with that boy," she says. "I'm sure it's spread through the whole academy by now. I just wanted to impart some of my wisdom to you."

I find myself blinking mutely. Does she think I'll get Wilder killed? He's a big boy, not to mention a vampire. I'm sure he can look out for himself.

"Treasure him for as long as you have him," she says. "You never know if your love will be cut short."

I have to resist the urge to snort. I've already spent too much time with Wilder. Something coming between us and cutting "our time short" would be a mercy at this point. But it would hardly further my cause to tell her that. So, I just smile and nod and hope that it looks like I'm taking what she said at heart. I set my bread down. "You know what, I just remembered, I promised Wilder I'd spend some time going over spells with him before our next class." It's a lie of course, but I suddenly feel exposed under Sofarynn's scrutiny.

I push to my feet, edging away before I quickly slip out the door. I hurry through the sunny courtyard. It's been quite sunny of late, usually the clouds hide the sun half the year so to have so many sunny days in a row is quite strange. I wonder what the vampires here think of it, but then I remind myself that it doesn't matter what these vampires think of anything.

The only vampires I should be concerning myself with are my father, mother, and sister. Not Wilder, not Professor Morozov, not any other vampire who may be hiding in the shadowy recesses of this city of stone.

The sunlight gently caresses my skin with warmth. I don't often wonder what it will be like when I become a vampire like the rest of my family. It's a certainty but one that is far in the future, especially since father is leaving the choice up to Natasya and I on when we are ready for it or not. But I find myself wondering what it will be like to never feel the sun again.

Someday its rays will harm me, they will not be welcome any longer. This will restrict my travel and my freedom in a sense. But my father has been a vampire for many years and my sister for far longer. They never allowed this state to get in the way of their ambitions. My mother became a vampire somewhat more recently; she held it off until she saw the first signs of aging.

She was worried that it would affect her ability to run the inn, but she seems to have settled into her new vampiric state.

So why should I be worried? Just because I'll never see the sun again?

I'll be gaining so many other things.

And yet somehow, I can't seem to find that thought very comforting. Perhaps I'm more like my mother than I give credit for. While I'm young, I feel immortal. It isn't until the first bite of age begins to ravage me that I'll go running to father and ask him to turn me.

But until then I just feel like running. I'm not sure from what. The future? My responsibilities to steal that spellbook? Sofarynn's allegations that I could destroy Wilder? Or the completely false accusation that I helped to create that I love him?

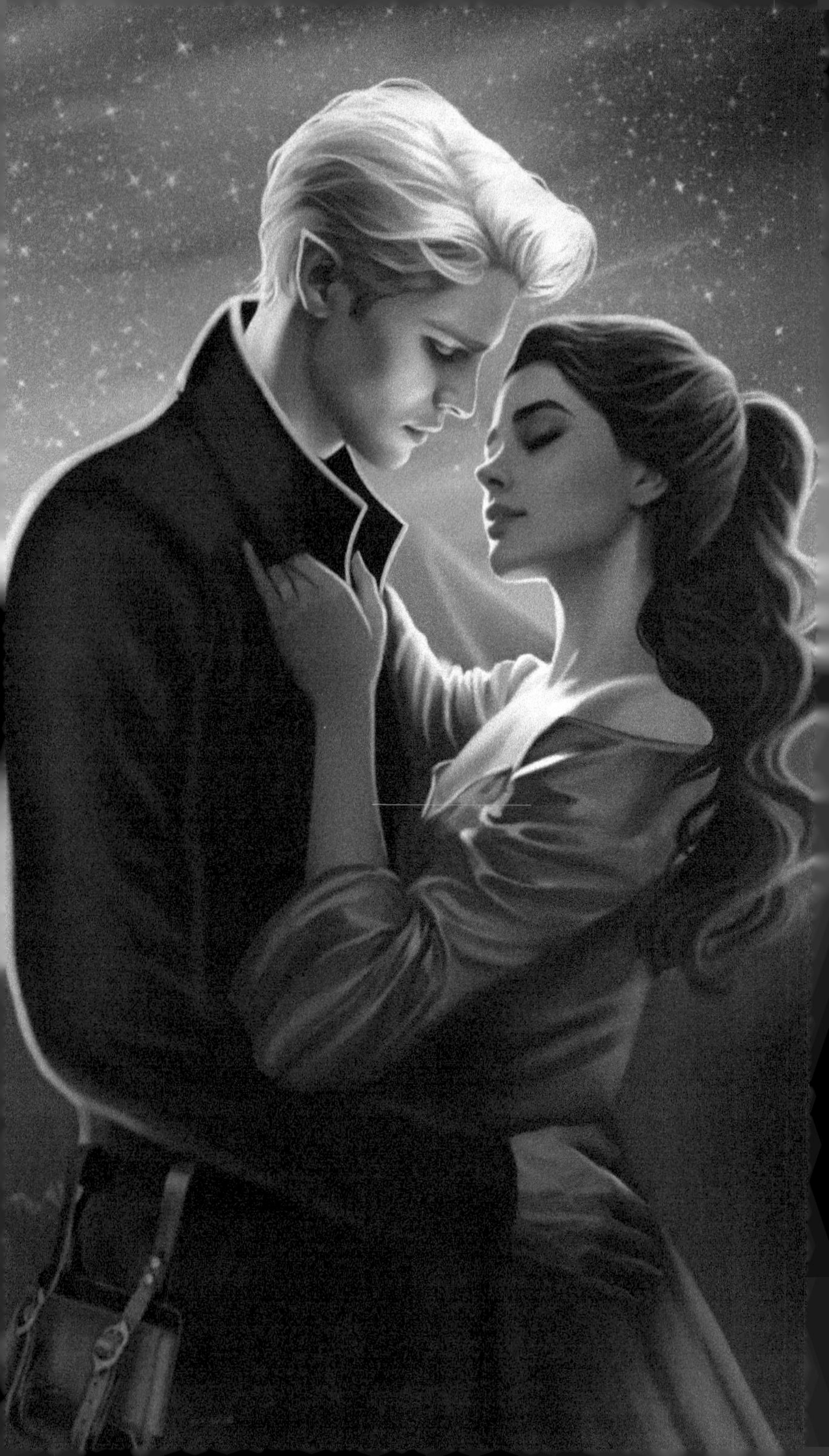

CHAPTER SEVENTEEN
BRONWYN

"There you are, it's a good thing that you're predictable. Otherwise, I might have spent all day looking for you." I glance over the top of my book to see Wilder make himself at home on the table in front of me. He lounges on it as if it is a cushioned sofa. "In a library, just like you, Eel."

"And how many libraries did you check before you found me?" I ask as I turn my page.

He purses his lips. "Three."

"And is there a reason you went through all this trouble to locate me, or did you just decide that I'd been enjoying my day too much and you had to do something to fix that?"

Wilder smirks as he rests his wrist on his knee, lounging back on his shoulder so that he has to roll his head to look at me. "What? Do I need a reason to seek out my fake fiancé? We're supposed to be desperately in love, you know. No one will believe that if we don't spend any time together."

I hold up a finger, pointing around the otherwise empty library. "No one is here."

His eyes flick over me as a troubled frown crosses his face. "And yet you're never around when there are people to witness it. Are you avoiding me?"

"Would you blame me if I was?" I ask with a sigh as I place my book down. I make sure to keep my hand placed between the pages, so I don't lose my spot. "Even if I didn't despise you, my life doesn't revolve around you. I've been busy."

Wilder goes limp, sulking into the table as he continues to stare at me. "I'm just trying to keep you safe."

"My life isn't presently in danger."

"That shows your naïvety, Eel. Morozov has been asking about you. Incessantly."

I roll my eyes at this. "He needs to get a hobby. One that doesn't involve obsessing over me."

"He's paranoid," Wilder hisses as he sits up. He glances around the room as if making certain that we are still alone. I wonder if any of that paranoia has spread to him. "And you aren't doing a good job at making yourself seem like you're not a threat."

"I've stayed away from him. What more do you want from me?"

"Would kissing me a time or two in the hallway really have killed you?" he grumbles.

"Very possibly, yes."

"Well, Professor Morozov wants to have you come to dinner," Wilder grumbles. "So not kissing me may have killed you. It depends on his intents." He slaps his knees. "Hopefully, you won't be *for* dinner."

I snort at that, and he narrows his eyes.

"You have a rather cavalier way of facing a reality of becoming a vampire's next meal."

"I'm not going to be eaten by any vampires," I reply coolly. "Besides, I just won't go..." I trail off as Wilder is already shaking his head emphatically.

His hair flies around his head with the force of his shake. "If you do that then you will be worse off than if you just submitted to his wishes now. Men like Morozov will tolerate you so long as they think they have power over you. You refuse him? Bronwyn, you would disappear."

I release a heavy sigh as I glance up at him. "If you're so scared of him, then why don't you do something about him? Eliminate the threat by taking care of him. I know someone you can contact if you need him... *discreetly* dealt with."

I trail off as I realize that I sound exactly like my father. I glance down at the table wondering why that idea scares me. I love my father, I look up to him, and yet I don't want to become like him.

Wilder swallows. I'm not sure how it is possible, but he pales even more so. "You want me to *kill* him?"

I bite down on my lip. Do I? Going to the proper authorities is out of the question, I can't afford to draw too much attention to myself. Assuming they would even believe me if I told them that a vampire had infiltrated their ranks and was now obsessively trying to figure out if I'm actually in love with Wilder. No, killing him would be the simplest option. Not that I intend to do it. I prefer to keep my hands clean unless I am left with no choice. And while Wilder is here and oddly bent on keeping me safe, I still have other alternatives.

I smile up at him as I rest my chin in my hand. "That's what I'm insinuating, yes."

"Bronwyn, I can't kill him. My father would... as much as I hate him, he is our partner. No, no, we can't do that. Promise me you won't do anything of the sort."

"You're really tying my hands here," I grumble.

"Just what sort of merchant's daughter are you?" he asks, sounding a little aghast.

I can't help but feel myself smile. I hope he is thinking about all those times he carelessly mocked me, it's a little nice for him to be now realizing that he was playing with fire by getting on my bad side.

I trace my finger over the cover of my book, not looking up at him. "I'd answer that only if you told me just what your father and Morozov are planning. And how you fit into it all."

"You know I can't tell you that. The less you know, the safer you are. You're already involved enough as is."

Finally, I look up, my eyes immediately locking onto his crimson gaze. "So, why not just tell me?"

He bites down on his lip but pushes to his feet instead of responding. "I will come and collect you at the dinner bell." His eyes flick over me and he sneers, once again slipping on the arrogant veneer that I know so well. "Please dress nicely. You're supposed to be pretending to be my fiancé after all, and I have standards."

He turns to leave, but I'm not letting him get away with *that* last word. I pluck my quill out of the little pocket I keep it in on the leather casing that holds my spellbook and flick it into the back of his head.

He flinches and turns glaring at me. "Madwoman."

"Monster," I spit back.

"I will see you at dinner."

"We will see about that, but just so you know I'll dress however I want."

He juts his chin into the air. "And I will find you contemptable if you do."

"Glad we understand each other then."

"As am I," he huffs, not sounding very glad at all. But then again, neither do I. With that he storms off leaving me fuming. A perfectly nice afternoon ruined and all just because Wilder had to show his smug little face.

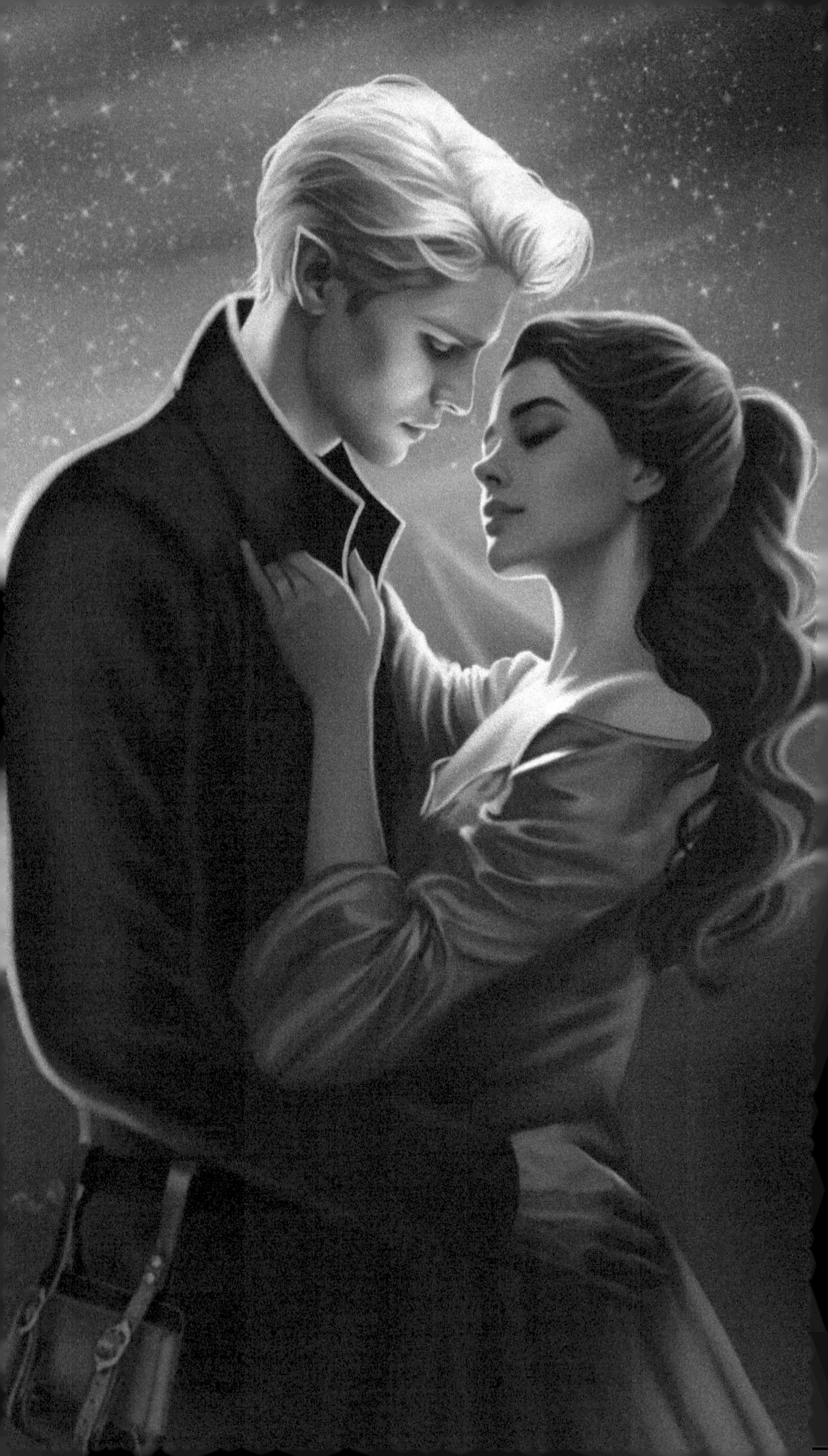

CHAPTER EIGHTEEN
WILDER

I'll be honest, I was almost not expecting Bronwyn to answer her door when I knocked. But there she is, in all her glaring brilliance. To top it all off, she's actually wearing an elegant gown, instead of buried in her bookish robes. It's a deep blue, naturally since that color represents magic most magickers refuse to wear anything other than the colors of blue and purple to show their status. But unlike her robes this one clings to her curves. It hangs off her shoulders leaving her neck and collar bone exposed.

She has a very nice collar bone, it's so elegant. Refined is perhaps a better word for it.

I blink twice when I realize that I'm staring and force my gaze up.

She raises a single brow. Her typically unruly curls are pinned back revealing strong yet slender features that are usually hidden behind them. Her brows, while thick, perfectly frame her eyes, drawing attention to their green depths.

Like a pool covered in moss that is catching the sunlight.

"Well? Do I live up to your *standards*, master vampire?" she asks, her voice dripping with contempt. "I'd hate to embarrass you by your association to me through our fake relationship."

Standards? Oh, she surpassed them. I'm suddenly worried that she will make me look drab in comparison tonight.

She cleans up well... for a merchant's daughter.

"You look passable," I admit at last, the words struggling to form past the lump in my throat.

Ravishing is a bit of a better word for it, but I can't have her getting too big of a head.

The glare is back as Bronwyn slips out of her room. Before she closes it, I happen to catch a glance inside. Like myself, she has one of the best, and most expensive, rooms in the academy set aside for her own personal uses.

While most have to share a common dorm, those of us with money are capable of pursuing our magical interests in privacy with our own runed circle for safe spellcasting without any destructive effects spreading. It's a large yet cozy space, but I notice that Bronwyn's room is bare. None of her belongings are strewn through it as if she never bothered to unpack.

There isn't even a photo on the mantel or a comb on her bedstand.

Or perhaps because she is keeping everything in one place for a hasty exit. Her room is that of a person who doesn't intend to stay long enough to unpack.

Such a thought should make me feel happy. I won't have to worry about keeping her safe from Morozov's and my father's plans if she just picks up and leaves.

And yet, instead, I am filled with an overwhelming sense of panic at the thought of never seeing her again.

I clear my throat as I try my best to compartmentalize those feelings just as I do with anything else I'd rather not be feeling.

I hold my arm out to Bronwyn, a gesture that she completely ignores.

"So, what exactly should I expect from this?" she asks stiffly as she starts down the hall. "I'm bringing my spellbook just to be safe. I hope you know that I intend to use it if Morozov makes a move against me, no matter how important he is to you and your daddy's plans."

"I hope you know that I would never lead you into danger." As worried as I am about the reason Morozov invited us to this dinner, if I actually thought he would try to kill her I wouldn't be bringing her. I was simply trying to scare her back in the library, I had thought that maybe if she's a little frightened she won't do anything stupid in front of the professor. But now the idea of her even being remotely afraid is too much for me. I want to pull her close and bury my hand in those tumultuous curls of her and assure her that she will always be safe.

It would be a blatant lie, I'm sure, I couldn't even keep myself safe from my father's plans, but I don't intend to fail again. I *will* protect Bronwyn, even if I couldn't do the same for myself.

"Do I know that?" she asks, her shoulders going stiff.

I reach out, grabbing her arm and halting her progress. She turns toward me, opening her mouth but I don't give her the chance to get out a sharp retort. "I hope so."

"Because you have given me *so many* reasons to trust you," she says, finally getting her retort out.

"I gave you my word."

"Something worth its weight in gold, I'm sure." Her tone drips with sarcasm. She pulls her arm out of my hold, looking like she is going to start going, but I put my arm against the wall blocking her path and successfully trapping her between it and me.

I don't care what she thinks of me, but she must know that I won't let anything happen to her. I want her to know that no matter what, she's safe around me.

She clenches her jaw but finally meets my gaze. I swallow hard as I hastily explain what I should have back in the library. "This whole dinner is because Morozov feels off-balance. He wants to exert control over me by forcing you to come. All we have to do is show up, play submissive, and let him have his power trip. It isn't about you at all, it's about controlling me."

"And whose idea was it to involve me by making him think he could control you through me?" she asks arching one of her perfect brows. "It was such a ridiculous notion that it's no wonder Morozov has a hard time accepting it."

"It's not so far-fetched as you make it out to be," I whisper, my eyes dropping to her lips.

She rolls her eyes. "Who are you trying to fool here, Wilder? We're alone."

I'm not sure what possesses me, the spirit of a demigod? But I find myself saying, "Good," and leaning forward. For the second time in my life, I kiss Bronwyn the Eel.

I'll be honest, I think the second time is more surprising than the first.

Last time, I kissed Bronwyn to save her life. This time? Well, this time I have no good reason. Honestly, I just wanted to, and her lips were right there and were so kissable.

I'm so surprised that when Bronwyn shoves me away, I am caught off guard and stumble back. Bumping the wall across the hall.

"What the jetting Skyhold was that?" she screeches, wiping her mouth with her sleeve.

I reach up, rubbing the back of my neck. Indeed, what *was* that?

"I, uh, that was just practice," I say, trying my hardest to school my face. I don't know what I'm currently feeling right now, but I don't want it playing across my face. Bronwyn is too clever; she would figure it out before I even have a chance to know myself.

Bronwyn glares up at me, her eyes sparking. She raises a finger, pointing it in my face. "We may be in a fake relationship, but this is crossing a line, Zubkov. You keep your kisses for show and only as a last resort. No more kissing in private."

I feel my eyebrows shoot up. No more kissing in private? Well, that's not so bad. It just means that I have to kiss her in public.

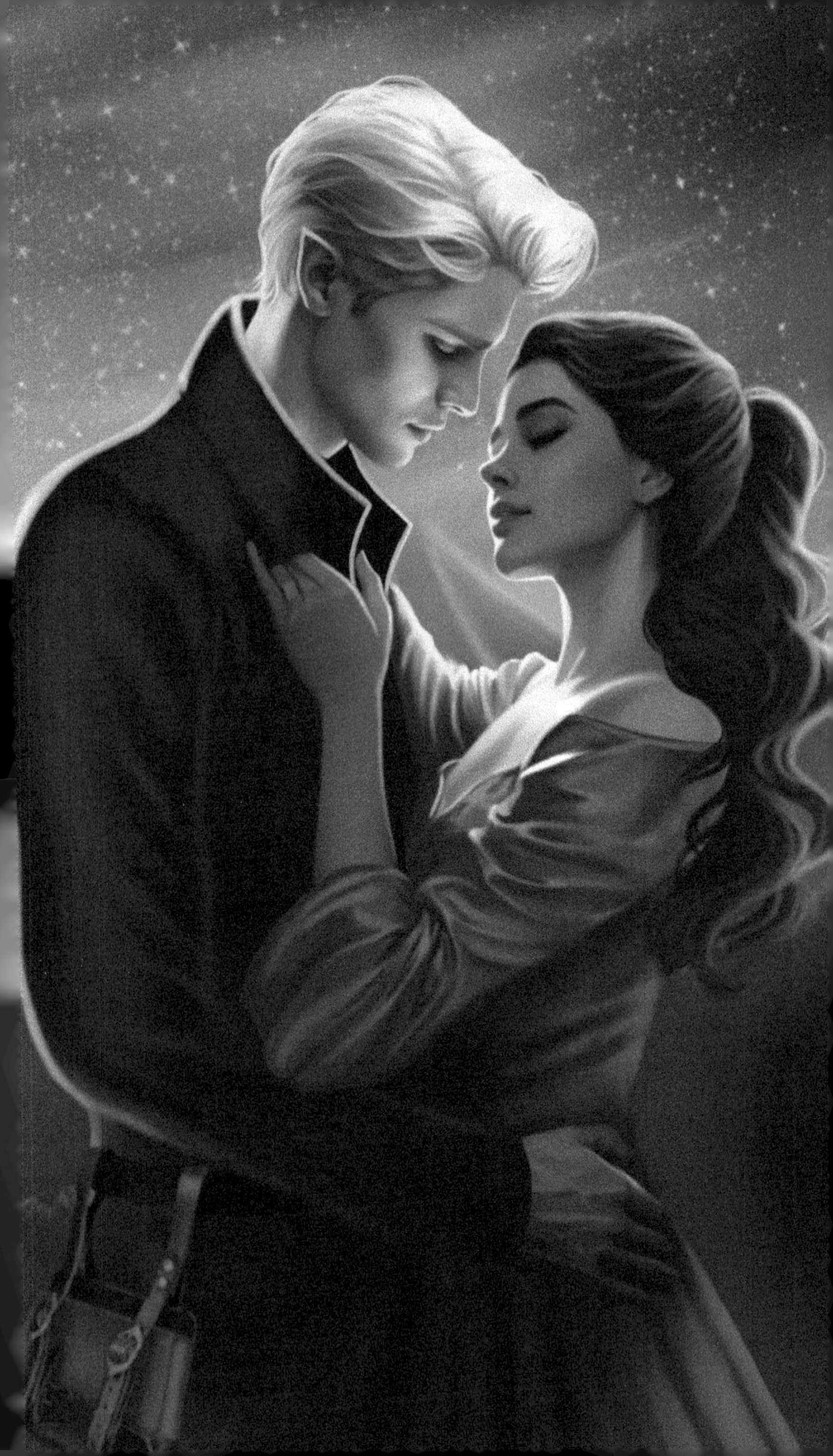

CHAPTER NINETEEN
BRONWYN

The kiss has played havoc on my ability to focus. My lips are still tingling and my heart races anytime I think of it.

I try not to dwell on the smirk that played across Wilder's face when I told him not to kiss me in private anymore. I know that he can easily work around that, he'll just kiss me in public. I could see in his eyes that was what he was thinking.

But I made that rule not so that he would stop kissing me. No, I made it to protect myself.

If he kisses me in public then I know it's all just a show, a part of our fake engagement. But when he pins me against the wall in a secluded hallway, looks me deeply in the eyes and then kisses me there, where there are no witnesses, what am I supposed to think?

That it was just practice?

Probably.

But it didn't feel like just practice to me. To me, it felt *real*.

Which is very, very dangerous because I am in no position to mistake reality for illusion. I don't like it when he looks at me like that because it makes me think that he might actually care. And with that thought I'm only setting myself up for heartache.

The last thing Wilder Zubkov will ever do is care about me.

I have very little time to compose myself before we are entering Professor Morozov's office. I run my clammy hands down my skirts as I glance around, taking it in. It looks very different from earlier this week, his desk has been shoved to the side and a long wooden table has been moved in with high backed chairs set up, two on each side.

I've never attended any of these banquets as a first year because honestly, getting to know my professors was the least of my concerns, but this isn't a wholly unfamiliar concept at the academy. It's a unique way for professors and students to bond, especially since we usually take our meals separately and only see each other in the classrooms.

There only being four seats is a bit concerning though, usually when a professor holds one of these his whole class is invited.

But the invites for this one seem to have been very selective.

And somehow, I made it to the list.

I swallow, glancing to Wilder for support before I remember that he is probably the last person I should look to for that. Still, he notices my glance and gives me a small smile. His hand reaches out, snagging mine, and he gives it a small squeeze.

I stare down at our interlocked hands unsure if I'm more shocked by the gesture or the fact that he hasn't released my hand yet.

I'm startled out of this line of wondering by the sound of a chair leg scraping against stone as it is pulled out.

"Please make yourselves at home," Professor Morozov says, gesturing to the table. "Our final guest will be arriving shortly."

Wilder raises his eyebrow; I can see the curiosity clearly written across his face. He has no idea who this fourth party is. He moves over to the table first pulling out a chair for me before sliding into his own, not staying to push me in. He has his chin resting in his hand a worried and confused expression written across his face.

I slide into my chair and turn glancing at Wilder, but I don't say anything until Morozov gets up to go over to a table across the room where he pours himself a glass of dark liquid that could be wine... or something a bit more sinister.

While he is preoccupied, I lean closer to Wilder. "What is it?" I whisper.

He shakes his head. "It's probably nothing, I just don't know who Morozov would invite for dinner unless it was..." he trails off, his voice getting thick. He is so unnaturally pallid, even for a vampire and when I look down at his hand, I notice that he is gripping the arm of his chair so hard that his tendons are popping out of the back of his porcelain pale skin. Without thinking I reach out, resting my hand on it.

"Who do you fear it is?" I ask rubbing my fingers across the back of his hand, trying to massage some of the tension out.

"My father," he says, stark fear flashing in his eyes at the word.

His father? The man is no student, why does he fear he will be visiting? He did not do so last year, but then Wilder wasn't wrapped up in whatever scheme this is last year.

I want to press him further, but just then Professor Morozov returns. So, I say nothing and settle for just giving his hand a light squeeze to let him know that I understand. I'm in this danger with him.

If his father is here, then he will reveal that I'm not actually Wilder's fiancé, and I very well may end up being supper after all. Now, that would be ironic. All my life I planned on becoming a vampire, but now am I to die at the hands of vampires because I put off becoming one for so long?

No, not while I have something to say about it. If I die then I doom my family, my father has always told us that his kind cannot survive a great heartbreak. While seemingly immortal Lower Elves are born with one great flaw, anything that they love, they cannot bear to live without. Not for all eternity.

And so, if they lose that love, they lose the will to go on.

They die from heartbreak, so to speak.

I will not be responsible for my father's undoing; I will not be the reason his empire falls. Not because of Wilder's father.

My other hand moves to my spellbook, I rest my fingers gently against it, right where the clasp is. I start mentally going through my memorized fire spells. Like most things that are semi dead, flames work the best in purging them from the world. Despite my interest in water magic, what are waves going to do? Wash them away?

That is why so many ignore water magic in favor of fire magic that is deadly and powerful and all too effective.

I will fight and kill anyone in this room who tries to touch me. I don't know if Wilder will help me, but I have to hope he will. In the very least, he had better not stand in my way.

He glances over at me out of the corner of his eye, and I try to discern what he is thinking and if he feels any true loyalty to me. Loyalty enough to choose me over his own father?

Not likely.

I notice his eyes dart down to my hand tapping a nervous rhythm on the cover of my spellbook. He stares at it for a second before looking away. His neck bobs as he swallows hard.

Before I can quite discern what I should make of that, there is a creak as the door opens. I turn, holding my breath, half expecting to see Wilder's father stride through the door, but instead I find myself starting into the familiar face of one of his two lackeys.

This is the thinner one, with the angular face as opposed to Asimov's fuller square shaped head and physique.

Gregos.

Or Wilder's shadow, as I have always referred to him. He always seems to be there behind him, ready to taunt me right after Wilder. I suppose I should have wondered where he has been all this time with Wilder being near me so much. But I didn't care enough to ask.

"Hello, Wilder," he says before his eyes flit to me. "Bronwyn, the surprise is all mine."

He smiles, flashing a smile of white teeth that are just a bit too pointed. His eyes in this lighting could be mistaken for deep brown, but I know that if I get closer, I would see the truth. His eyes are red, like the blood that now sustains him.

Wilder doesn't seem to notice the minute changes to his friend. I suppose it's fair, he did not grow up in a world of vampires like I did. He was only recently thrust into this world. And so, despite being a vampire himself, he is slow to pick up on the signs.

"Gregos?" Wilder asks, turning a clearly questioning gaze to his friend. "What are you doing here?"

"He is here," Professor Morozov replies in his stead, "because when I informed him of your recent engagement, he simply would not believe me unless I showed it to him. I'm surprised that you failed to discuss this engagement with your closest friends," Morozov continues in a slow tone, obviously challenging him.

"Gregos would know if he had showed up the last time Asimov and I had a drink," Wilder says coolly. "I would have broken the news to him then just as I did for Asimov, but he was unwell." Wilder pushes to his feet as his eyes flick over Gregos. "I am glad to see that you are better now."

"Better than ever, my friend," Gregos says with a smile. "Although that is no thanks to you."

Wilder raises his eyebrow. "If you are going to accuse me of getting you sick, you had might as well save your breath. I've been in perfect health."

Gregos glances at me, before he leans closer to Wilder. He raises his eyebrows. "We may be in the academy of Meruna, but you and I both bear the gifts of night do we not?"

Wilder's eyebrows furrow as he tries to make sense of Gregos's words. It's simple really, he is referring to the Lady Night, the demigod daughter of Neltruna, the goddess of darkness and monsters. Lady Night is the mother of monsters, considering that she birthed the first dragons, and her followers were the first vampires. The rivalry between the mother and daughter is bitter indeed and followers of Neltruna are usually self-proclaimed vampire hunters.

But I suppose Wilder wouldn't have too much knowledge of the demigods, not since their worship is illegal. He was not raised by a necromancer like I was. My father laughed in the face of worship of the gods. He and my sisters all serve the demigods instead.

I suppose I'm more of a neutral ground because I chose to pursue magic which was instituted by the gods instead of sorcery that the demigods wield. But I chose magic, not the gods.

But Wilder was likely raised on very little information on the demigods. He doesn't strike me as particularly devout either, so I doubt that he spends much time in temples worshiping the gods and learning their stories.

Wilder's eyebrows furrow as he tilts his head. "What are you... *night gifts*?"

This time Gregos looks straight at me as he says. "I have been welcomed into the order of monsters, my friend."

I stiffen, feeling my mouth drop open that he would so brazenly say such a thing in front of me, but then I notice Morozov watching me intently. Almost hungrily and I realize that this was always his intention to reveal this part of his secret.

He is testing me, seeing how I will react, and that reaction will determine my fate. In their eyes anyway.

The only problem is I'm not sure what reaction they expect me to give so that I can mimic it.

Fortunately, Wilder has enough of a reaction that it draws all the attention from me for a time. He stumbles away from Gregos, the back of his foot catching on the end of his chair, causing him to fall while the chair makes an unholy screeching sound as it is shoved to the side. I step forward in a vain attempt to catch him, but instead he catches himself on the table. His hand lands on a platter which sends lettuce and a roast pig flying all over him.

The pig drops to the floor, just as Wilder whirls on Morozov. "What have you done?"

"My purpose here," the professor replies calmly. "I went through your notes and selected the best."

"And you didn't consult me first?" Wilder grinds out. "He was my friend."

"I still am," Gregos says as his eyes flick to me. "I just happen to understand you better now."

Wilder turns to him, his nostrils flaring before he reaches out grasping my arm. "Come, Bronwyn."

His hand trembles slightly when Morozov barks. "Where are you going, boy? I am not done with you."

"But I am with you," he snaps out before he strides forward, dragging me after him. We are running by the time we reach the door. I'm tripping on the edges of my fancy skirts to try to keep up with him. I'm not sure if he is running from Morozov and Gregos despite the fact that they don't chase after us... or if he is just running from the thoughts in his head.

And if that's the case I don't have the heart to tell him that he won't succeed in doing that.

I should know that more than anyone. No matter how hard you run, you can never escape your own mind.

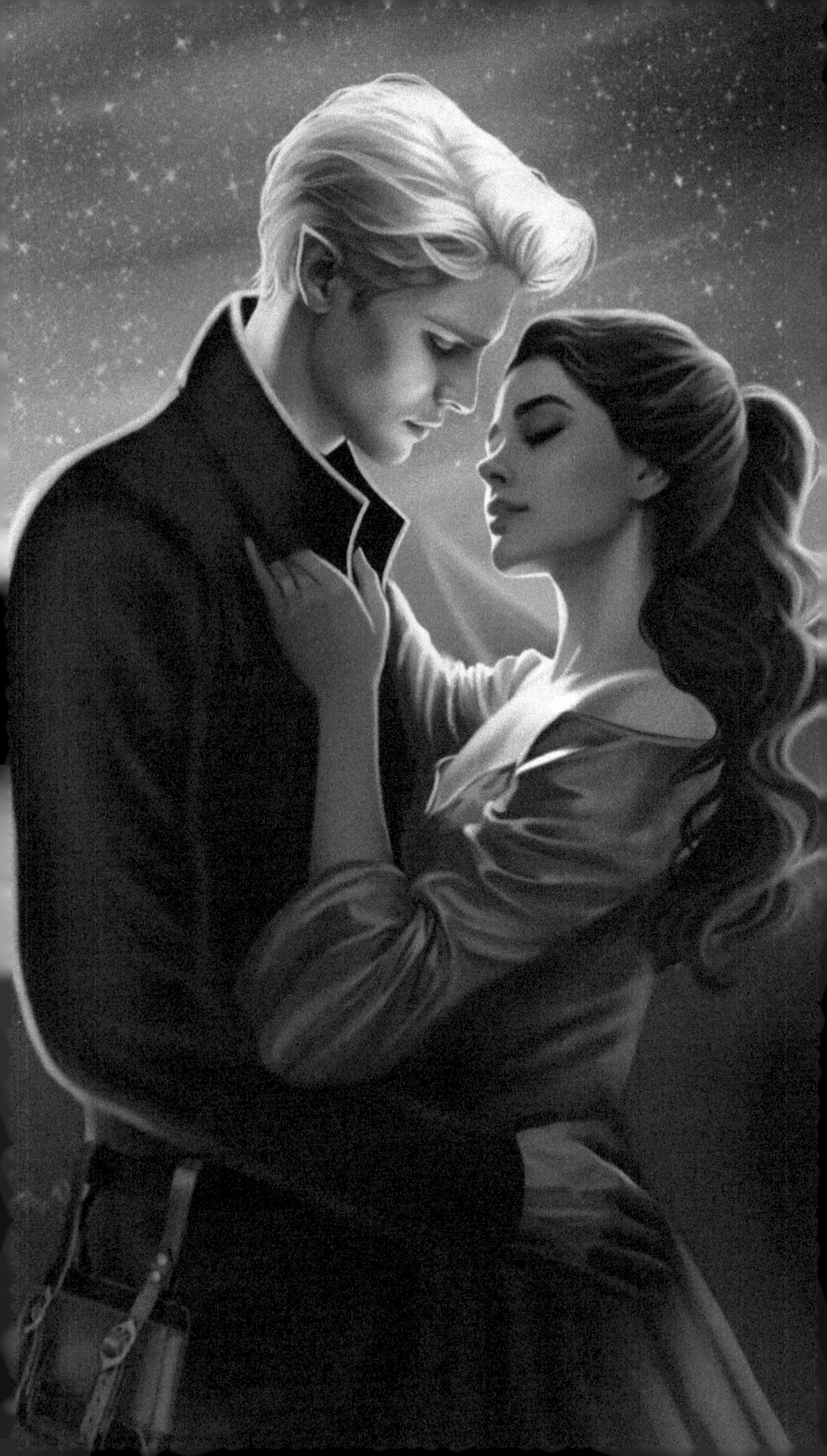

CHAPTER TWENTY
WILDER

I collapse against the wall, heaving for breaths and shuddering. I can't seem to get my trembling limbs under control. I don't even know what wing of the academy we are in now. I just ran blindly in my panic. I'm surprised I had the presence of mind to grab Bronwyn before the urge to flee overtook me. Otherwise, I would have left her behind just as I ran away leaving behind all reasonable thought.

Gregos... my friend.

Asimov had said that he wasn't feeling well, but I hadn't thought anything of it. I still remember my transformation so vividly still. How Morozov arrived at my manor a few weeks before the break ended. My father said that it was for the best. Then came the bite.

I spent three days bound to my bed, tormented by feverish dreams and then I awoke as *this*.

It was the worst, most horrid experience of my life. I would give anything to go back and save my younger self from this fate. But there is no known cure for vampirism.

And now Gregos is its victim as well. And I'm just as at fault for his fate as Morozov.

All this time I've played a complacent partner in his plans, trying not to think of what they will mean. After all, they were my only hope for normalcy. So, I made the selfish decision to keep my eyes and mouth shut to what Morozov was up to.

I chose to save Bronwyn, protecting her was a boon on my guilty conscience.

And all the while he was turning one of my only true friends into a monster. While I stood dumbly by and let it.

Morozov may have been the one to bite him, but I'm the one who made Gregos into a vampire.

Liquid streams down my cheek but I'm unsure if it is sweat or tears. Then suddenly a hand is on my shoulder. It gently wraps around me, pulling me close. Her other arm wraps around my middle, and I feel her chin on my arm.

She hugs me in spite of the lettuce stuck to my spellbook and the grease staining my robes. Probably ruining her beautiful dress.

She doesn't say anything, and for that, I am grateful. She just holds me until I stop shuddering. Then she slides to the ground with me as I drop to my knees, worried that they will give out on me if I stand any longer.

She finally releases me as I turn with my back to the wall. We sit there shoulder to shoulder for a while. I don't know for how long, but I'm grateful that she doesn't try to use my weakness to pry me of my secrets. Although, I'll admit that it leaves me with the odd desire to share them all with her regardless.

"My father forced me," I rasp out, surprised by how raw and husky my voice is. I am too drained to lift my head away from the wall, but I do turn it enough to take her in as she's sitting next to me.

She presses her eyes shut, her long lashes brushing the top of her cheek. She gives her head a little shake. "You don't need to explain anything to me."

"I *want* to," I say firmly. I want to finally be able to tell someone. I feel the silence that I have been forced into clawing at my throat, begging me to keep it, but I can also feel it eating away at me. Rotting my insides and leaving me as nothing but a hollow husk. "I want to."

She slides her hand across the stone floor, her fingers extended toward me. I move my hand toward her, our fingers tangling. That warmth gives me the strength I need to push through.

"I always knew that my father was a hard man, not the kind of man you messed with. Not even if you were his son, but I'd never thought... the extent..." I give my head a sharp shake as I try to block out the memory.

The sight of my father standing in front of our hearth, a stranger next to him. He smiled at me, he never smiled at me, and then he beckoned me forward.

He told me that it was time I started meeting his business associates.

And then he introduced me to Morozov.

"He has plans, such horrid plans for this world," I choke out.

Her fingers press into mine, and I swallow. "I don't know how long he has been planning this with Morozov, but they intend to create an army of vampires from the students of this academy. One by one they will turn them just as they did to me. I was the first."

"How could they think they could get away with something of this scale?" she demands, finally speaking up.

"That's where I came in. I was supposed to find the most powerful, wealthy, influential students and bring their information to Morozov. He would start to build his vampire army from the best of the best. Anyone who would stand against us we would crush and all else would be forced to join us. They wanted the whole academy before the year was out."

"Those papers you were writing," she murmurs. Then she turns to me. "But after he turned them into vampires, he would have no control over them. Why did he think he could turn so many against everything they had ever known? They have friends and family that surely, they wouldn't want to harm by becoming part of a vampire army?"

"He planned to play on their desperation to belong. You have no idea what it is like to have your humanity taken away from you. You have nowhere to turn except to the monster who made you this way. Vampires are hunted, Bronwyn; none of us can exactly go to the authorities. That is what he was banking on. He would do something irreversible to us all, and then promise a world we could live in without having to hide. With the promise of acceptance, he would control them all. It's how they controlled me." My voice catches in my throat and I take a moment to clear it. "After they turn us into vampires, we will do anything for that promise. At least, that's what they were betting. And I certainly did not let them down because even though I hated my role I felt I had no other choice. Once the era of the undead had begun I could finally be what is normal again. Even if the new normal is facing life as a vampire."

"But that could never work," Bronwyn says sliding her hand from mine. She pushes to her feet and begins pacing back and forth, her anxiety apparent. "There is a whole world outside this academy. They would have stopped you."

"Who can stop an army of magickers?" I ask with a snort. "Not anything I know of."

"You would have been trapped within these walls and others like it," she says, slapping her hands against her hips. "Vampires cannot rule, not while the sun is in the sky. You will always be regulated to prowling at night and hunted during the day."

I hold up my finger. "But that's the beauty of their plan. We are in the Academy of Magickers and once they have it at their disposal, they will also have all the magic they need to overcome their weaknesses. Although there is only one magic Morozov says he needs. Water magic."

Bronwyn goes so pale that for a second, I wonder if she was bitten and is now a vampire. "Water magic?" she breathes.

"His specialty. His obsession, more like," I snort in disgust as I think back to the hours, I had to listen to Morozov ramble on about it. "He swears that there is a spellbook written by a long-dead magicker who mastered water magic which will help him attain what he wants."

"Petrov Hansimov," she mumbles so quietly that I can barely make it out.

"Yes, that does sound familiar. Morozov says that this man was more powerful than any magicker here today, that he once created a storm that covered the whole of Ruskhazar. Morozov wants to recreate that storm. Blot out the sun with the clouds and rain. Then the third era will end," I say with a shrug. "He is so obscene he wants to create a fourth era, the era of monsters."

Bronwyn looks down at me, her face is still but I can see a thousand thoughts racing through her eyes. "How does he intend to get Hansimov's spellbook?"

I lift my shoulder in a shrug. "Probably by turning the guardian of it into a vampire and forcing her to work for him for her own survival. It's his plan for most things."

Bronwyn lunges forward, I blink in surprise, but she simply drops to her knees in front of me. She clutches both my hands, holding them up in front of us. "Wilder, we need to get this book before he does. Will you help me?"

I hesitate only with my mouth but already I feel myself nodding. At this point I'd do anything to stop Morozov's plan, even if it comes at the cost of my future of never having to hide from the sun again. "I—yes. But how are we going to do that?"

"I have a plan," she says as she pushes to her feet. Then she turns away and starts down the hall, seeming to believe that's all she has to say to get me to join her.

She's right, but I'll expect a full explanation later.

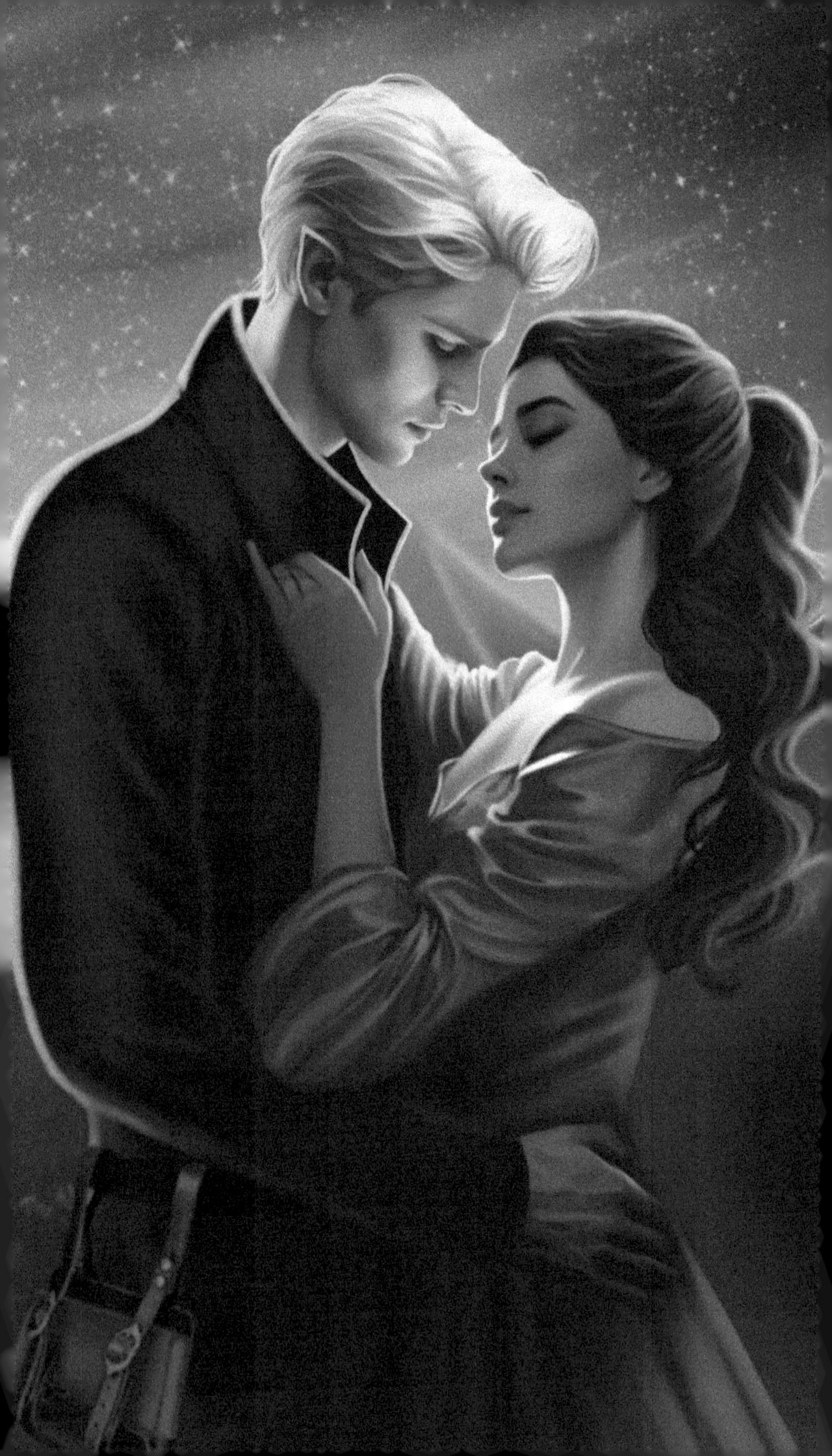

CHAPTER TWENTY-ONE
BRONWYN

I should have pressed Wilder harder from the start. I should have done anything I could to figure out Morozov's intents. I had thought him a devious vampire, certainly, but I had no idea his plan stretched this far. To take over the academy by turning everyone within into a vampire?

To blot out the sun?

I am used to conniving vampires; I was raised by one. My sister is another. My mother is a recent addition. I suppose that made me underestimate just how evil Morozov was because I never saw vampires as inherently evil.

I was always just so focused on my own task of gaining that spellbook. Wilder and Morozov were mere curiosities and annoyances—each in equal measure.

But I was blissfully unaware that if Morozov had his way he was going to snatch it from right under my grasp and turn me into a vampire in the process. Ahead of my time.

"Where are we going?" Wilder demands as he takes in the entrance hall to the building. The hallway opens up to a high vaulted ceiling with a massive stained-glass window above the doors that leads out to the courtyard of the academy.

I wonder if Wilder has stepped through these doors at all since arriving here. Being a vampire can greatly hinder your freedom, and I doubt anyone taught him the tricks my father learned to continue existing in the daylight. To wear layers and cloth masks pulled over his face to protect himself from harmful rays that would threaten to boil his skin.

Fortunately for us, it is night so there is nothing stopping Wilder from being able to enter the courtyard. I shoulder open the door and glance at him. "I thought you could do with some fresh air."

His mouth twists in disbelief. "We aren't leaving the academy, are we?"

"Not in a manner of speaking," I reply as I start toward the wall. The shadows of the night, normally my fellows, feel threatening. Where is Morozov? What is he planning? Does he still consider this a grand game, or has he decided to move up his timetable due to our reactions at dinner?

All I know is that I don't intend to be dismembered tonight. Or any night really. It's a policy that I tend to try to stick to.

However, we make it across the dark courtyard without any problem. The northern lights flicker ahead, reflecting on my hand as I raise it to knock on a door built into the wall.

It takes a few knocks before Sofarynn opens the door, stifling a yawn. Despite the late hour, it doesn't appear that I woke her from a sleep. She's dressed in her everyday robes, and her curly hair is no more disheveled than usual.

She pauses when she sees me. "Bronwyn?" her eyes move to Wilder, and confusion clouds her features.

"May we come in?" I ask, twisting my ring.

She opens her mouth but then snaps it shut and moves out of the way. I step into her office and slide into my usual seat. Wilder follows me in, his arms crossed tightly. He looks Sofarynn over. "You're the keeper of the books?"

"And you must be Bronwyn's fiancé," she replies as she shuts the door. I wince slightly at her words and move my hand up to massage my brow. Right, everyone still thinks we're engaged. The world is under the threat of an eternal storm in the sky, and people think I'm going to marry Wilder Zubkov. This is not what I was expecting when I came to the academy at the start of this year.

Wilder presses his lips together as he leans forward resting his hands on the back of his chair. "I see my reputation precedes me."

Sofarynn's eyes flick over Wilder as she purses her lips. "Why have you come to my room in this manner so late at night?" she asks as she wraps a portion of her robe more tightly around herself.

"I need your key," I reply rubbing my finger over the arm of my chair. I look up at her. "The one that leads to Petrov Hansimov's final resting place and where his spellbook lies."

I can't believe what I'm saying, a whole year of trying to get her trust and I'm throwing it away by just outright demanding the key?

Oh, my father would be so disappointed if he saw how easily my artfully crafted plans are just thrown out.

Sofarynn squints as she takes me in, her eyes darting to Wilder. "What are you—?"

"I need Hasimov's spellbook," I state, cutting her off.

"That's something I never thought I'd hear in my lifetime," she says with a small laugh. The smile slides off her face. "You realize I can't just hand it over to you, right?"

I push slowly to my feet. "Surely, you don't agree with it being locked away, the pages rotting, never to be read?"

She purses her lips. It appears that I struck a chord.

Perhaps my time in her company was not so wasted, after all, I know enough about her to know that she cherishes books as if they are an appendage of herself. It's something she and I have in common.

Wilder taps his finger against the back of my chair. "I may not be the best person to say this, but also if you don't give it to us, you will likely be turned into a vampire."

She whips her head to Wilder, her mouth opening as if she will scream. He holds up his hands. "Not by me. But others will not stop at stooping to such unscrupulous means."

Sofarynn's eyes flick over Wilder, likely finally taking in the slight alterations to his coloring that are commonly missed at a first glance. She shakes her head, leaning on the desk. "Great, first werewolves and now vampires."

I want to ask what she means by werewolves, but I'm too focused on getting that spellbook. I lean forward, almost out of my chair as I look at her, pouring every ounce of earnestness I have into my gaze. "Name your price, my father will pay it."

"I don't need money," she replies with a shake of her head.

I suppose I knew that already. She wouldn't be living in these dingy quarters as a lowly bookkeeper in the academy if she was searching for money. I bite down on my lip as I press further, "My father is a powerful man. He could give you anything you asked."

She gives her head a small shake, grief filtering across her expression. "There is only one thing I would desire and that is beyond anyone's grasp."

I assume she is referring to her blacksmith. Technically my father is a necromancer, but that only works with the body. It cannot bring back the soul. She would probably consider it a sacrilege for me to even mention it.

"Although..." she begins. She looks up at me, a spark of cunning filtering through her somber eyes. "My brother lives a quiet life. But there are people looking for him. Of late, they have been getting too close, asking too many questions. If your father can do anything about that..."

I straighten as a bit of hope shines into my soul. I try not to sound too eager as I say, "As a matter of fact, that happens to be his specialty."

After all, I'm still agreeing to something unseemly. Sofarynn trusts me enough to even consider giving me the key. I don't want to scare her off by my inability to flinch at shady deals.

"To clarify, I don't actually want anyone dead, but if they happen to disappear forever, I will rest easily knowing that I at least said that."

"I will pass that request on," I say although I think we both know that it won't be honored. There is only one sure way to make certain that someone disappears forever. "What is your brother's name? My father will get to work immediately hunting down his hunters."

Her mouth turns up. "His name is Taliz."

"Taliz?" Wilder whispers. "You mean, like the champion of Coldhaven?"

Sofarynn's smile says it all. I feel my jaw drop open. It's true that Taliz was an exile, he had a sister that the tales often paint as a villain. But I never actually assumed he was a real person. I thought it was a wonderfully spun tale and nothing more.

Taliz is what is sung in my mother's inn, not an actual person. Or so I assumed.

But I guess I shouldn't be so surprised. If my father is a vampire crime lord and the leader of a reclusive family of assassins, then surely men who burn villages to save them can also exist.

Wilder starts spluttering.

"I'm going to trust you," Sofarynn says with a heavy sigh.

My mouth drops open, and Sofarynn snorts. "Don't look so surprised, or I might just change my mind. The gods know I shouldn't but... you're right. That spellbook deserves to be read, the spells within deserve to be cast." She rests her hand against her chest. "Not by me, of course, I cannot wield magic. And even if I could, I promised Snorre that I would never pursue forbidden magic again after losing him."

I glance at Wilder, pressing my lips together to try to keep from showing too much excitement that would cause her to realize just how desperate I am for this spellbook. My father always taught me to temper my emotions when striking a deal. If someone sees that you are willing to do anything for something, then they might get the idea to ask for anything.

Wilder, however, looks too stunned to speak. I suppose I cannot blame him. It isn't every day that you meet the sister of a legend.

Sofarynn lifts a necklace off from around her neck and sets it on her desk. "I ask that if you find something interesting to tell me about it. I do love hearing about magic, even if I can never touch it."

She turns to her desk, grasping a few books before she turns away, striding toward the door.

"Where are you going?" I demand, pushing to my feet.

She arches her brow. "To see my brother. One time is enough to be a pawn of a power-hungry immortal, I think. If there are truly other vampires involved, then there is nowhere safer I can be than at his side." She nods to me. "Be careful, Bronwyn. I pray that your pursuit of this forbidden knowledge ends better for you than it did for me."

Then the only friend I made here at the academy walks out into the night. Leaving behind both me and her key as it sits on her desk, glistening in the candlelight.

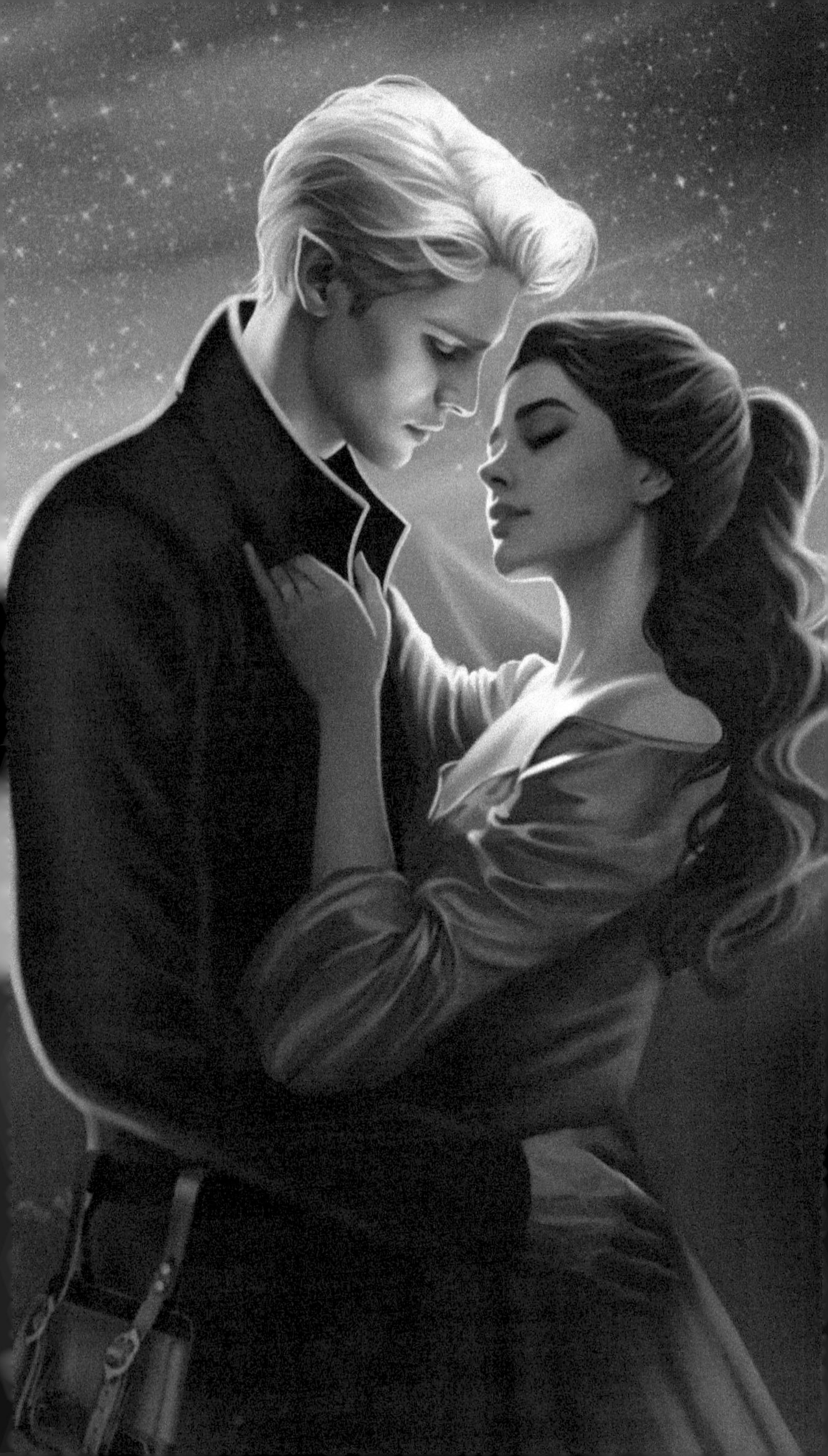

CHAPTER TWENTY-TWO
BRONWYN

I know exactly where Petrov Hansimov is laid to rest. Truly the only thing that had been standing in my way was getting Sofarynn's key. I was always worried I'd have to find a way to steal it, indeed I think my family wondered why I hadn't stolen it in my first year.

But instead, she gave it to me willingly. All I had to do was ask. It makes me wonder if all those afternoon meals spent with her finally paid off.

Or perhaps she saw something in me that I didn't see in myself... something that lead her to believe that I'm actually a good person.

That I'm not taking this book for myself to help further my father's criminal empire. Or maybe she realized she had no choice one way or the other, and she decided to remove herself from the equation.

After all, her last home burned, and it was blamed on her.

Bards still sing about it to this day.

How weary she must be after everything she has lived through. Perhaps if I were in her shoes, I would have done the same thing. I suppose I'll never know because to me this key is more than just a key, it's something my father told me to retrieve and if there is one person in this whole godsfrosaken peninsula I don't want to let down, it's him.

He gave me my life, he gave me hope, and a family.

I'd steal all the spellbooks he required of me.

The keyhole is a small nick in the stone at the base of a fountain to the east of the courtyard, easily ignored if you didn't realize what was lying underneath.

Hansimov, like all the rest of the founders of the academy, was buried in tunnels underneath the city of stone. None of the other founders' tombs have actually been found, save for Hansimov, but that's fine because according to our best knowledge, only Hansimov was buried with his spellbook.

My sisters have been tasked to find the other spell books, but I was sent to collect the one known to be at the Academy of Magickers. Since the rest of my family are sorcerers, I'm the only one who wasn't in danger of being branded as a heretic.

I drop to my knees next to a still pond located at the edge of the courtyard. There is a statue at the center of the pond,

Hansimov himself. It's probably why his tomb was found and those of his fellow founders were not. Hansimov was apparently ostentatious.

I mean, I suppose one would have to be to adopt the title of Lord of the Seas in a landlocked mountain range. Ostentatious or downright mad, but that doesn't mean that his magic is useless.

After all, blotting out the sun to create a vampire paradise is just one possible application for this magic, and once I get my hands on that spellbook, that will be my father's power.

My own power since technically I'm the only member of my family capable of wielding it. I will be his arcane master and finally have a place in his criminal empire.

Natasya can knit a monster out of the bones of men, making an unkillable army.

Corallin is like a shadow, unseen and unheard with all the skills of a master assassin.

And me? Well, I can read a spellbook without being cursed by madness.

There is a clicking sound as I insert the key, followed by a rumble as the statue shifts to the side, moved by some hidden mechanics within. Underneath the statue I can make twisting stairs that spiral downward.

I glance at Wilder and smirk. "I guess there is nowhere to go but down."

He swallows hard as he looks at me, speaking for the first time since we left Sofarynn's office, "Who are you exactly, Bronwyn the Eel?"

I push to my feet ignoring his words. I hike up my skirts so that they do not trail in the shallow pool as I step through it to reach the statue. I peer downward. There is an opening below, wide enough to fit a narrow spiral staircase that is so tightly packed in that I cannot see beyond it.

"I'm not asking that question rhetorically," he says coming up beside me. "I'd truly like to know. You know all my deepest secrets now; I think it's only fair I know yours."

"It wasn't a trade, Wilder," I reply muttering the first glow spell I can think of off the top of my head. It's the one that I used in Morozov's office. Just a small orb that follows me. When it comes to basic spells simplicity is best. Why would I have need of a light that shines a different color or for a set amount of time?

No, I need only memorize one singular light spell and worry about mastering more complex spells in more useful fields of magic.

"I still want to know," he mutters morosely.

I feel myself smile. I'm sure he does. I look over at him. "All you need to know is that I will take that spellbook far away where Morozov will never be able to use it." Hopefully, that will at least stymie his plans for vampiric conquest.

That's the best I can offer the world.

I am no hero. I just have my own uses for that spellbook.

Wilder's hand lashes out faster than I can blink, clamping down on my arm. I turn back, first taking it in and the cold seeping through the arm of my sleeve from his touch. Then I raise my gaze to him. "Wait, you're leaving?" he demands.

I find myself mesmerized by his crimson red eyes. So brilliant that the northern lights highlight them even in the night. They are like twin rubies that would be found in my father's treasury.

And they shine with desperation.

I swallow before I force myself to nod. "Yes, I—I—will have gotten what I came here for. There would be no reason for me to stay."

Indeed, it would be too dangerous for me to remain. Not just because of Morozov, but because the theft of the book might be traced back to me.

I pull my arm, but Wilder's grip is unyielding. "But..." he whispers.

"But what, Wilder?" I demand as I yank again. This time he releases me, and I fall down two steps in my surprise before I'm able to catch myself. But not before I manage to scrape my arm fairly badly. I hold it and glare up at him. "But what?"

He blinks, glancing away. "But nothing, I suppose," he mutters as he passes me a handkerchief. "Now cover that up, you reek of blood, and I haven't eaten for a few days."

I snatch the handkerchief from his hand as I press it against my arm, disappointment welling up within me. I don't know why I should be disappointed. Yes, there is something unspoken between us. Something that neither of us are willing to say out loud. But it is better for it to remain unspoken. To say it would make it real.

Unspoken I can pretend that I am imagining the longing look he throws my way. I can assure myself that my heart does not break just a bit at the thought of saying goodbye to him.

I can try to pretend that what I feel toward him is loathing plain and simple.

That the kisses were all a part of a ruse that we put on to buy us time.

But if he admits what I fear he is thinking then I will no longer be able to ignore it. I'll know beyond a shadow of a doubt that our fake relationship got too real. For him as well as me.

And I don't know how to deal with the consequences of that. I quickly turn and start down the stairs, keeping my hand on the wall as I follow the downward descent toward the sound of rushing water.

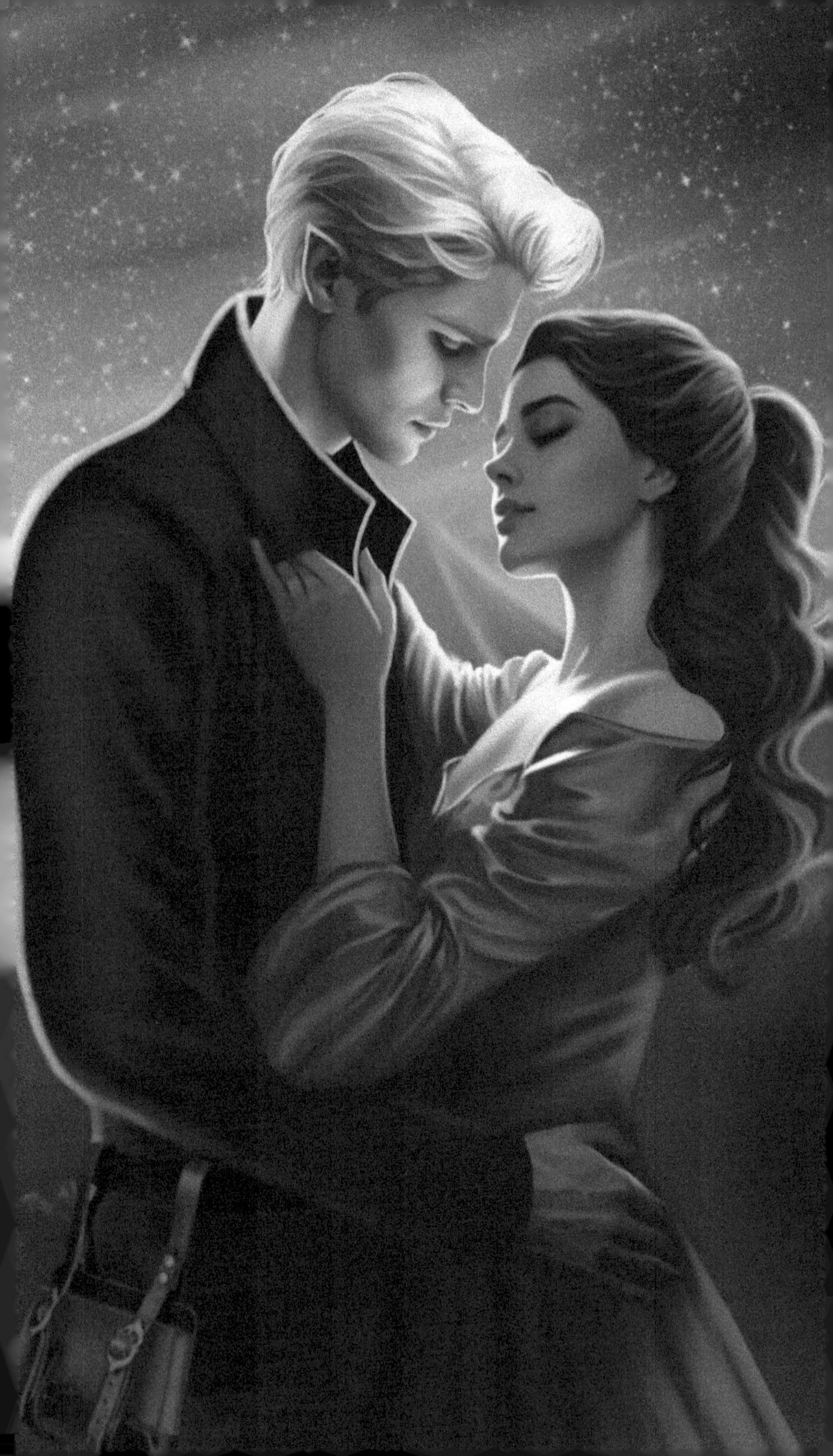

CHAPTER TWENTY-THREE
WILDER

I am capable of accepting the fact that I do not deserve happiness. I'm a bleeding coward. I never stand up for myself nor have I fought for *anything* that I have ever wanted. I allowed myself to be turned into a vampire because I never stood up to my father and put an end to his abuses before they left this irrevocable change on my person.

I didn't do anything about Morozov. I considered him an unwelcome pest more than anything, until he turned my friend into a monster.

And then there is the whole mess with Bronwyn. And now I'm unsure what I could possibly do to make it so that I no longer feel as if my insides are being ripped apart.

No, I do not deserve happiness; I've never in my life done what is right, either for myself or anyone else. I've only ever done what I was told.

But even if I don't deserve happiness, I still don't enjoy physical discomfort. And the fact that my boots are wet is really just an injury added to insult. My ankles feel as if they have been rubbed raw and every time I lift my boots, the water sucks at them as if I am fighting invisible hands grasping my foot.

"Jetting underwater stream," I mutter under my breath. Since we've reached the bottom of the stairs, it's as if we have entered a different world entirely. One where water is the ground on which we must walk.

I reach out a hand, steadying it on the curved wall. Waves reflect on the stones giving it the appearance of moving.

Bronwyn has since given up trying to keep her skirts dry and instead allows them to trail along behind her as she makes her way through the cavern ahead of me.

I try not to allow my eyes to linger on her for too long. It just reminds me of all that happiness I'm not permitted to have.

The coward's way, that's my path already well-worn and eked out with a lifetime of terrible choices.

A monster unfit for love. That's what I am, and the problem is I was that before I became a vampire. After all, if I was fit to be loved, would not my own father have seen that in me?

I clear my throat, desperate to revoke those thoughts. I don't enjoy dwelling on my father for too long. There is only so much I can handle of his harsh glares and stern reprimands, even from my memory. He tolerated me because he had to, I was his heir after all. But obviously he still saw me as expendable enough to force me to become a vampire and an unwitting pawn in the Academy of Magickers, while he remained a safe distance away with his humanity intact.

He had a way out if Morozov's plan failed, and I'm literally dooming myself to a life underground in a cavern just like this one, devoid of this woman who has enthralled me into her willing pawn.

I look up, taking in her cascading curls before I let out a drawn-out exhale. "I'm sorry, you know?"

Bronwyn whips her head around, arching her brow. "Is this where you reveal you have double crossed me?" Her tone is jocular, but I notice how she stiffens.

I trip slightly, sloshing through the water before I reach out to steady myself on the wall. "What? No. I simply meant for how I treated you last year."

The truth of the matter was I was a bit of a monster before I ever became a vampire. I think if I'm truly honest with myself I would admit that I have always felt this draw toward Bronwyn, only last year experiencing it made me angry.

I was furious that I would feel this way toward a mere merchant's daughter. I could never be with her; my father would not allow it. So, I took out the frustration I felt toward the inferiority of her birth and my own inability to stand up for what I wanted on her.

If I couldn't have her love then I would at least have her hate. But now that she does hate me it just leaves me feeling hollow.

"Oh," Bronwyn says, sounding taken aback. "I—well, I suppose you are forgiven."

Forgiven. She says it somewhat flippantly as if it is not my atonement.

I tilt my head as I step toward her, my hand trailing the damp stones for balance. "So, what does that make us? Are we friends then?"

"I guess, all things considering..." she trails off before giving a nod. "Yes, friends."

Her words are like a blow. I don't actually want to be her friend, but I suppose I'm still just the same man I was last year because I'm willing to settle for a little something over absolutely nothing.

"Never quite had a friend who made me feel the way you do," I muse out loud.

Bronwyn whirls, nearly losing her balance. Her lips part in a question I don't give her the chance to ask.

"So," I say quickly to change the subject and hide my crumbling heart. "After you have this spellbook what is next for Bronwyn the Eel?"

I know what my future looks like and it's depressingly bleak.

She studies me, the light bobbing next to her head throws her face in shadow.

"Obviously you aren't intending to become a magicker," I say wincing as my boot rubs up against another blasted sore spot on my foot. "So, if a life as a freelance magic wielder, selling your spells to the highest bidder isn't in your future... what is?"

Bronwyn turns back around and starts down the tunnel without a word. For a while I think she's just going to ignore my question, but at long last she finally just shrugs. "I guess I'll go into the family business."

"The merchant business?" I inquire. "Or are you alluding to your mother's inn?"

"Neither, let's just say... my family is a bit more than meets the eye and leave it at that."

Even though she is facing away from me, I can hear the smile on her lips as she speaks of her family. "Are you close to them?"

"Very much so," she replies without hesitation.

"That must be nice," I murmur. I kick at the water. "My father and I rarely see eye to eye. He's a harsh man that always expects perfection and compliance."

Bronwyn glances over at me again, her eyes sparking with sympathy. "And your mother?"

"I think she loved me. My father sent her away when I was quite young, he said I was adopting too much of her culture as a Higher Elf. She was just a servant so when he let her go, she was forced to seek employment elsewhere. I like to think that she writes to me sometimes and that he just confiscates the letters before they reach me."

Bronwyn has stopped moving, I draw to a halt just behind her. Without a word she reaches out and snags my hand. She gives it a squeeze as if she is trying to will her sympathy into me. If only she knew that I don't want her sympathy.

I'm not sure what I want from her, but sympathy certainly isn't it.

She starts forward again, and she doesn't drop my hand, so I'm forced to keep close behind her as we make our way down the tunnel.

"I love my family," she says in a heavy voice. "But sometimes I feel as if I am growing up in their shadows. As if they fill too much space and that there is no room or need for me."

"I can't imagine a world that has no need for you," I say, her words causing a jolt of surprise to run through me. How could she say that she loves her family when they make her feel inferior?

How could she even feel inferior? What sort of amazing talents must her family have to make someone as truly exceptional as Bronwyn the Eel feel inferior? She's the smartest person I know, sharper than a blade, and beautiful to boot.

She ducks her head, and I'm quite certain that I don't miss a slight rosy color tinging her ears before she raises her hand. "Look, the tunnel widens ahead."

Indeed, it does, I'm not sure why she felt the need to point it out.

After all, I have eyes to see.

I also have ears to hear, and I can make out the sound of rushing water just beyond.

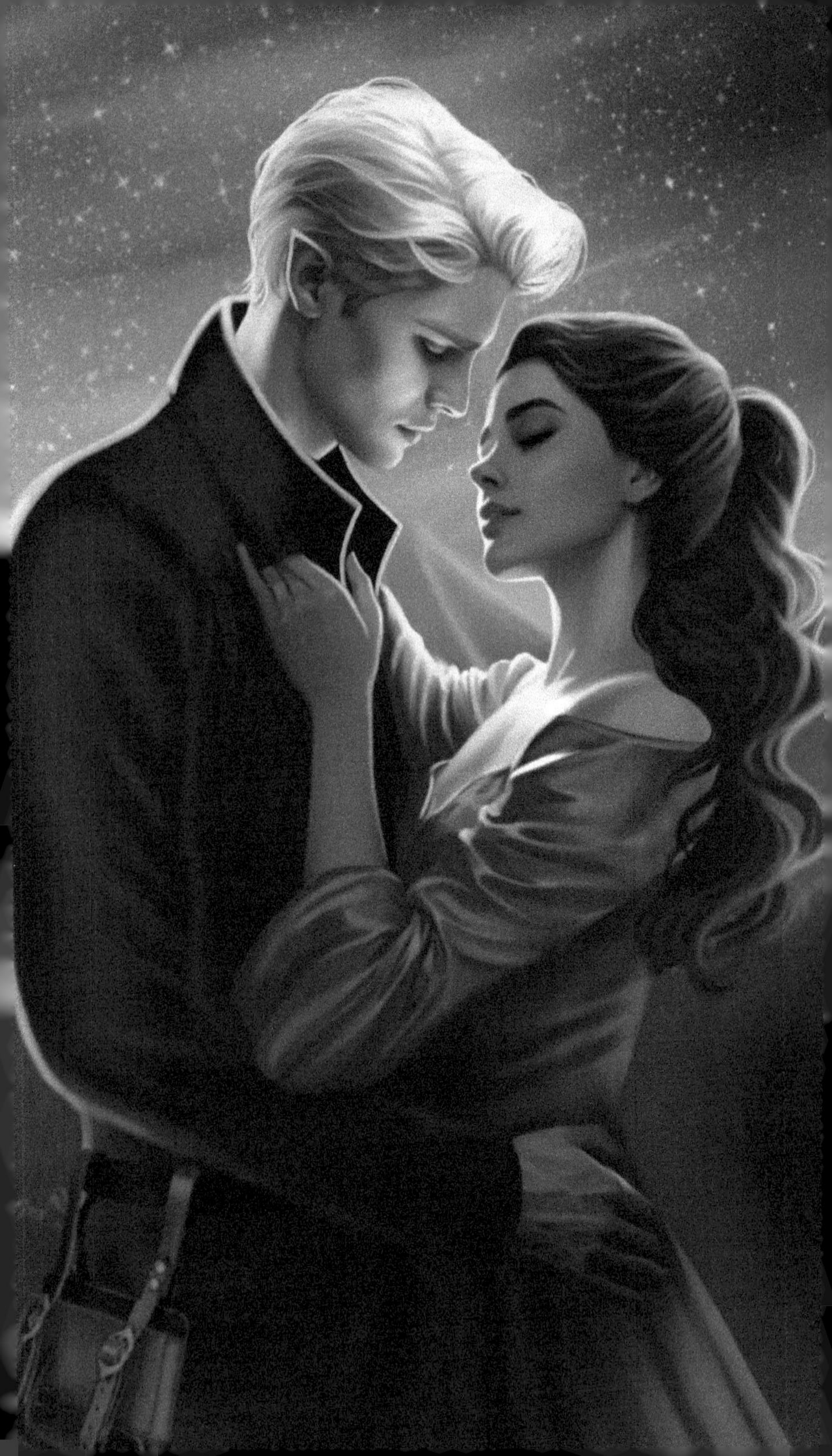

CHAPTER TWENTY-FOUR
BRONWYN

The room I find myself in as I exit the tunnel exceeds my wildest expectations. I have never seen anything like this, and my father's lair is set in a half-crumbled city built into a mountain, a remnant of the Higher Elves' societies before their great collapse that left them as outcasts.

Even with the wonders of that architecture and knowing how deep and vast underground chambers can be, I still find myself utterly stunned by what I behold. Dozens of waterfalls cascade down from hidden sources in the domed ceiling far overhead. They land in water that is green as if it belonged to the sea, churning and bubbling up, but the water toward the center of the room is crystalline and blue.

There is a single platform in the center of the room and on a raised dais is a rectangular box.

The resting place of Petrov Hansimov.

Mist rises up along the corners of the room, but the water surrounding the platform is entirely smooth. Uninterrupted by the churning waves surrounding it.

"This really is something," I breathe as I take it all in.

"If I ever die, make sure I'm buried in a place like this," Wilder says, his tone equally awestruck.

It's with a great effort that I force myself to lower my gaze. It lands on the dais. "The spellbook must be lying with Petrov in his tomb."

"And this is where I must interrupt you."

I startle at the loud voice ringing through the vast chamber, louder even than the roaring of the waterfalls.

I whirl to see Morozov standing behind me with a twisted smile on his face. Gregos is next to him, his arms crossed and a hard expression on his face.

"What?" I ask stumbling back a step. I glance at Wilder, wondering if maybe he double crossed me after all. I knew he was being suspiciously kind to me. He even apologized for bullying me and fool as I was, I believed him. But he looks just as befuddled as I am. "How?"

"You foolish girl, did you think that I would just allow you to walk free knowing our secrets without my reasons?" Morozov lets out a laugh that echoes through the room. My ears have started ringing. "I haven't trusted you from the start, and for clearly good reason. So, I watched you.

And I saw that you spent an undue amount of time with that bookkeeper… *Sofarynn* was that her name?"

I glance again at Wilder, edging away from him.

"So, you decided to use me?" I ask.

"I decided you must have designs on the key. So I bided my time, I knew if I got Wilder upset enough he would tell you my plan, spilling his guts like the stuck pig he will be if he doesn't get back in line, and then it was only a matter of waiting for you to open the door and lead me straight to the very spellbook that is essential for my conquest of this world."

I move to the center of the path, blocking the way to the tomb with my body. If they want it, they will have to go through me. Or start swimming, I suppose. "Not if I have anything to say about it," I spit out.

Wilder throws me a glance full of terror, but Morozov only laughs. "Ah, Bronwyn the Eel, I have been looking into you, trying to figure out why you also want my book. From the outside your father appears to be a respected merchant, and the owner of the only successful inn in Ruskhazar. But at a deeper look I realized that things did not add up. Business partners disappear, competition disappears, so, so many disappearances are linked to your father. Did you know that your father's inn is the only one that has not had some calamity befall it?"

He takes a step forward, but I hold my ground, my eyes darting to Gregos.

"They say that inns are cursed here in Ruskhazar, and yet your father's is thriving. And his competition? Burn down, the owners are killed, food winds up with poison in it." He tilts his head. "So curious. That tied in with the many accidents in the shipping industry. Dangerous work, especially with the supposed reawakening of the krakens and yet the men dying are not the sailors. Instead, the danger lies with those who had any sort of say in your father's business?"

"I'll have you know that the inn is actually owned by my mother," I reply tightly. "It was a wedding gift."

"And yet the point still stands." Morozov smiles. "The atrocities I discovered that happened to landowners before your father bought their land do not even bear speaking."

"And yet you bring it up anyway."

"All I'm saying is that I know what type of man your father, this *Elwis the Eel* is. He is a man who exists in the shadows of life, he wields so much power and I would suspect that he carries even more power in the criminal realm of Ruskhazar than even I realize. I must have an audience with him."

"Bronwyn, what is he talking about?" Wilder asks, shifting a nervous glance toward me.

"My father does not grant audiences to men like you," I say ignoring Wilder.

"He will when he hears that I have his daughter."

I cannot help it, I snort. "That's a death sentence."

Morozov rolls his eyes. "Oh please, you won't be harmed. I'm sure I can convince your father to see reason. Especially when he sees you a vampire by my side." Morozov raises his hand, his palm up. "Come with me, together we will blot out the sun and usher in a new age. The elves and men have had their time to rule, now it is time to bring about the era of the undead."

I back up a step; my eyes darting from Morozov to Gregos who has begun to circle around so that I can only face one at a time. My back bumps Wilder's chest, he must have moved behind me when I wasn't preoccupied with Morozov. I turn to look at him.

"Zubkov, this is your chance to be a man," Gregos calls. "Bite her."

My fingers move down to my spellbook as I watch Wilder's neck bob as he swallows.

"Don't do this, Wilder, you're better than this," I hiss.

"Ironic that you will tell me who I am, but I have no idea who you are. Who *are* you, Bronwyn?"

"I—" I begin but then I swallow. I'm my father's daughter, how can Wilder truly know me if he doesn't know my father?

Wilder shakes his head, confusion and betrayal shifting across his expression. He backs up a step, moving another one before he turns and takes off running toward the center of the room.

"Wilder!" I shout.

Before I can move to stop him, I spot Gregos moving out of the corner of my eye. I whirl, pulling my spellbook out of its special leather holder in my belt, opening to the page inscribed with my fire spells. If these vampires think they can take me, turn me into one of them, and use me as a hostage against my father then they are sorely mistaken.

And then after them, I'll have to figure out some way to deal with Wilder Zubkov.

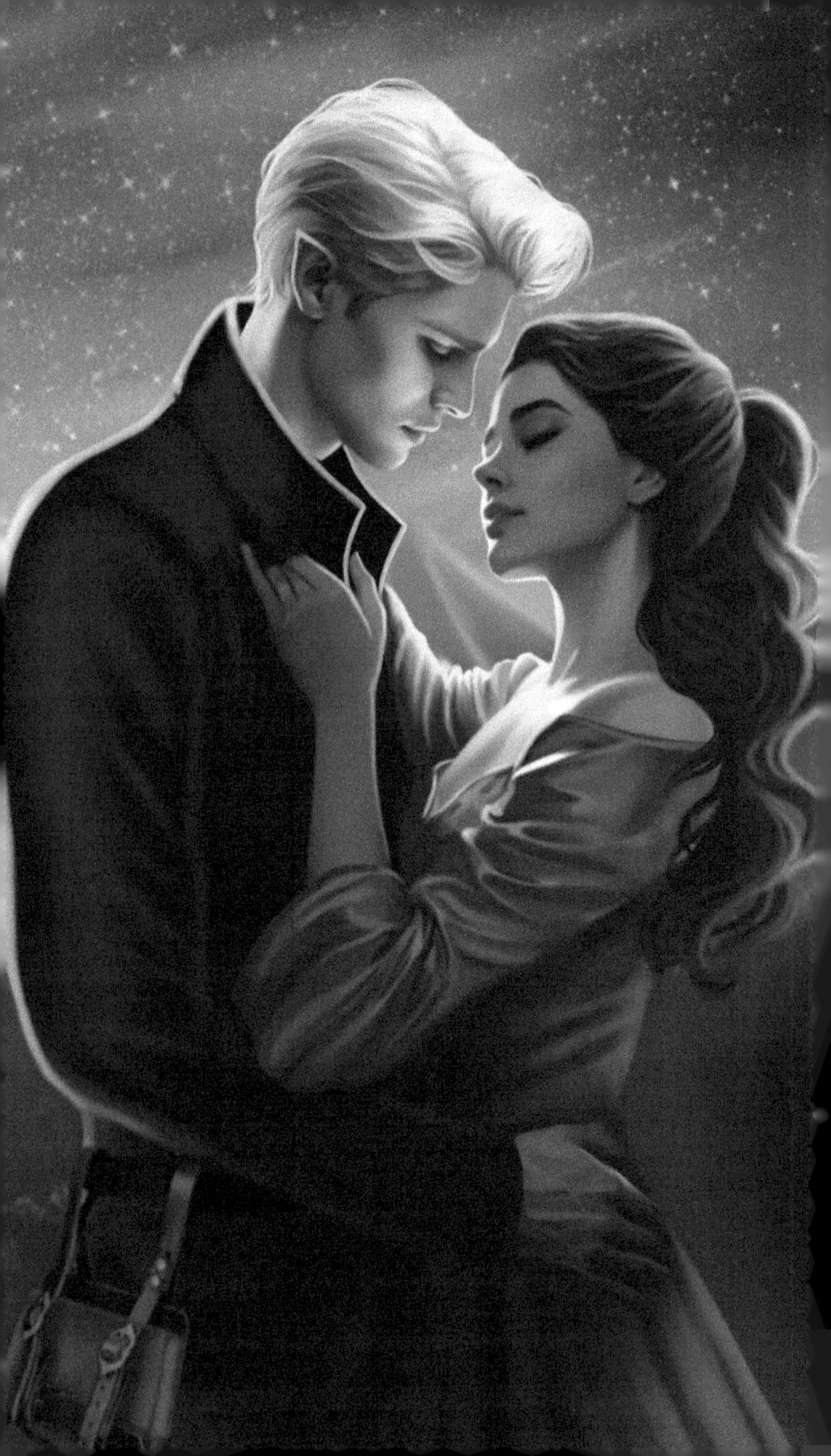

CHAPTER TWENTY-FIVE
WILDER

A blast of heat meets my back. I look over my shoulder to see that a wall of flames rising up in front of Bronwyn. Her silhouette nothing but a dark form with flapping skirts.

But Morozov is a professor of magic, and he did not become one by being easily bested in magical battles. As soon as that thought crosses my mind, a rushing wave of water crashes into Bronwyn's wall of flames, snuffing it out and leaving that half of the room enshrouded in mist.

I turn back around and pour on the speed as I race toward the tomb. I skid a bit as I try to stop next to it, my boots having difficulty finding traction on the wet stone.

I brace myself against the tomb. It's an intricately carved coffin with runic markings etched into it around a carving that is likely supposed to be the likeness of this Petrov.

I mutter a quick apology for desecrating his grave and pull out my spellbook, summoning a gust of wind between the lid of the coffin and the base. At my command, the lid goes flying off; the massive stone crashes to the floor and splinters into three pieces.

I wince and mutter another apology before I look over my shoulder, trying to see what is going on. All I can make out are flashes of light and crashing waves.

I turn back to the body within. At this point in decomposition, nothing about it looks remotely human. The skin, while preserved to the best of the abilities of those who entombed it, is stretched across the bones. Only scraggly bits of hair remain, clinging to the dried husk. I wrinkle my nose in disgust before my eyes lower to the bright purple book lying clutched under two skeletal hands.

"So sorry about this," I mutter before I pause. Why do I keep apologizing to him? He is dead; it isn't as if he cares what I do anymore. Petrov is in Skyhold. He will have no idea what happens here in Ruskhazar.

I grit my teeth and grab the spellbook. It doesn't at first budge, so I have to yank it. There's a splintering sound, and the spell book comes free with so much force that I nearly fall backward. I hold the book up and almost let out a cry and throw it when I see that there is still a hand attached to it.

However, at the last second, I manage to get control of my trembling limbs. I shake the book so hard that I dislodge the hand. It drops to the ground, and I shudder as I turn to the book in my hand.

The cover is worn with the edges frayed, and the symbols marking the front worn away, but those are the only signs of its age. Other than that, it seems to have held up remarkably well. I can only hope that I can say the same for myself after a thousand years.

I quickly flip open the book, my eyes scanning over the pages, but I can't quite believe what I'm reading. Because these pages are telling me to wield magic like sorcery.

But that can't be, that's impossible. Sorcery and magic are two separate entities. They have separate sources; one comes from the goddess Meruna, and the other the vile demigods. Mortals bend magic to their own will by controlling it with spells while sorcery is at its source the demigod's power that the heretics only channel through themselves with the hope that their demigod overlords will heed their wishes.

There is no one alive capable of wielding both together. Sorcery and magic can never mix, and those that try either die in the attempt or are driven mad by it.

But perhaps the most practical difference between magic and sorcery is that sorcery can only manipulate that which is already there, whereas magic creates anew. The flames that Bronwyn is wielding, she is creating from the magic she wields and the same as Morozov with his water magic. He is creating new water, not using what is already in this room. That's something only a sorcerer would be capable of.

I may not have been the most diligent of students at the Academy of Magickers, but I know enough to realize that.

And yet that's exactly what this book is telling me to do. At least, it is telling me that instead of creating water with magic, that I should imbue the qualities of the water around me with magic. That such an act would cause it to obey my spells as if I had conjured it myself.

Down the passage I hear Bronwyn let out a short scream that is quickly cut off. I lift my head, gripping the spellbook more tightly. I don't have time to deliberate on whether this is sorcery or not.

If it is then I will just be cursed because I'm not about to allow Morozov to do to her what he did to me. No matter who she may actually be underneath all the lies.

Coward as I am, I could never let her share my fate as one cursed to be a vampire. I draw the line at that happening to the woman I love.

Love.

The word shudders through me, causing a ripple in my emotions like a wave. I find myself smiling. So perhaps I know so little about her past. I know enough about her that I will never actually allow anything to hurt her. And I know enough about myself that I am irrevocably smitten.

Even if she isn't just a merchant's daughter.

I start back toward the entrance of the tunnel muttering the spells within the book under my breath.

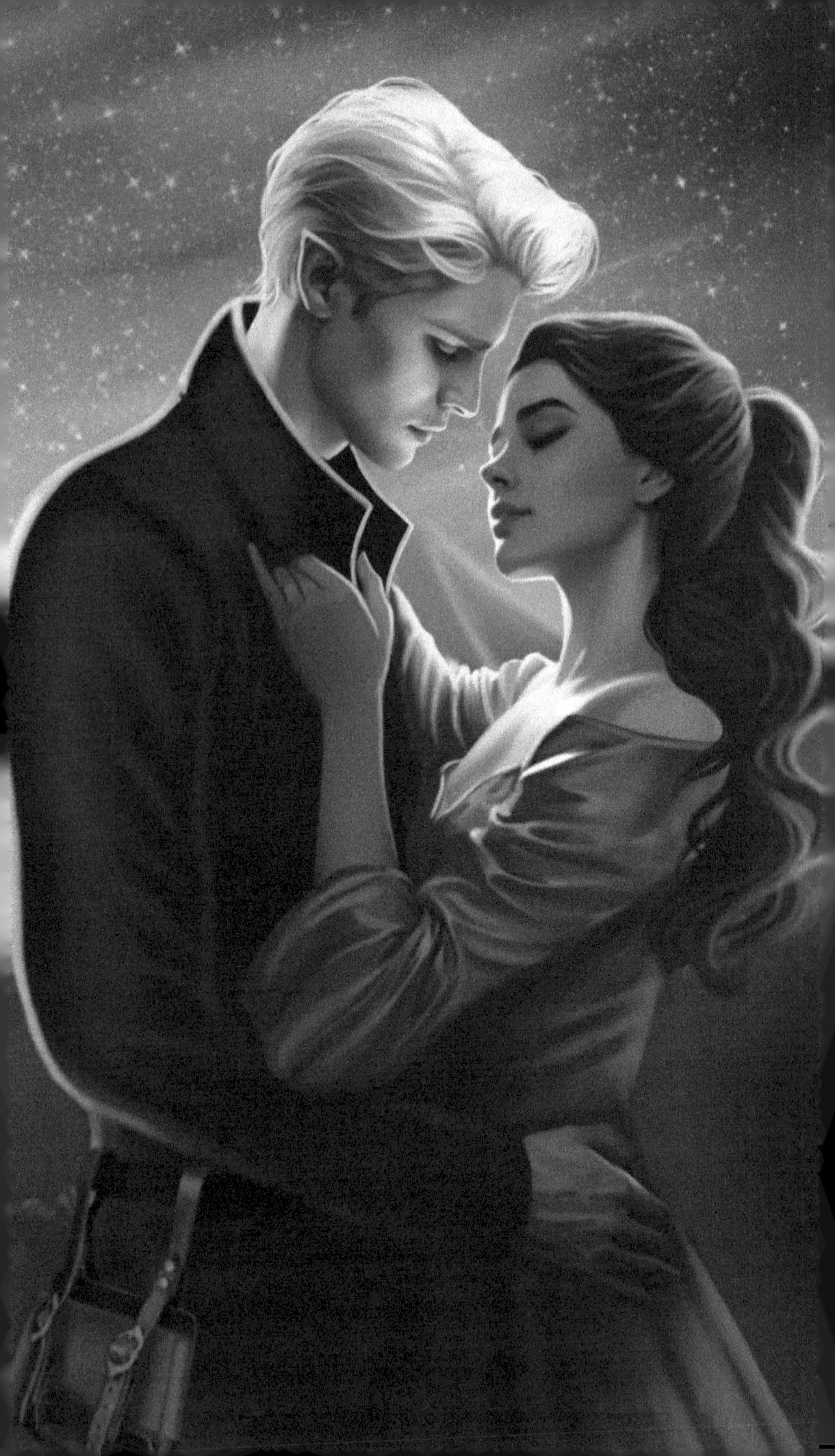

CHAPTER TWENTY-SIX
BRONWYN

Morozov's boot bites into my wrist as he presses on it until I'm forced to release my spellbook. I stare at him as I gasp for breath; my head throbs from where I hit it when he knocked me to the ground with a blast of water that struck me square in the chest.

A true magicker would not be so useless without their spellbook, they memorize a myriad of spells for if they are ever caught without it and yet in this very moment all my hours of studious study desert me. My mind is blank as I stare up into Morozov's crimson eyes.

I'm sorry, Father, I failed you.

Morozov turns his head, looking up at Gregos. "Get the spellbook from Wilder. It's time he decides which side he is on once and for all."

"No need," I twist my neck to see Wilder's black boots step back into view. I'll be honest, I'm surprised he is still here. I thought he was going to bolt the second Morozov was distracted by me. Save himself.

So why does my heart jolt so unexpectedly that he is here? I don't even know that he hasn't completely abandoned me. He's probably just going to hand the spellbook back to Morozov and go back to being his unwilling lackey.

However Wilder smiles as he fingers the pages of the book in his hand, cockiness exudes off him in a way that I have never seen. Not even when he would recount his lofty magical heritage and how much money his father has. "I already picked a side, and I'm afraid you're not going to like this, but it isn't yours, Morozov."

Morozov hisses in disgust as he applies more pressure to my wrist. I feel the bones strain under his boot. "You fool, you are going to betray me after everything your father and I have put into place for you? You could be a prince."

"A prince of vampires?" Wilder asks, his tone dripping with contempt. "I'm not quite sure that's the award you believe it to be. Now, kindly get your foot off my fiancé before I remove it for you... and from you."

Morozov clicks his tongue in disappointment. "That was the wrong answer."

"And your time abusing my patience is up," Wilder says. Then his lips move, I can't quite make out what he is saying, but he is clearly casting a spell. Most magickers learn to utter their spells in only the barest of whispers to make sure that their enemies do not overhear it and steal their spells.

"You're a fool if you think—" Morozov begins but he is cut off by the sound of rushing water. I crane my neck to see the waterfalls shift their position, instead of falling downward their waters come flying toward us. There's nothing Morozov can do to stop it. Magickers can only control the objects they create with their own magic, and yet... Wilder is turning the very waters in this room against the other vampires.

The waves wash over us, sweeping over Morozov and Gregos, but creating a bubble of air around me as if it has been commanded to not even touch me. In a second, they are gone, washed away, and thrown against the opposite wall. Then the water recedes, slinking back into the pools around us.

I sit up gingerly glancing over at Morozov who is slumped against the wall, Gregos beside him. Then I turn to Wilder who is standing there with droplets suspended in the air around him, a half crazed look in his eye.

I push slowly to my feet, my feet splashing puddles as I move cautiously toward Wilder. He doesn't move as I raise my hand to cup his cheek. He blinks, and when he opens his eyes, they shift so that they are staring at me.

I draw in a shaky breath before I swallow. Slowly he reaches up, grasping my hand turning it over, studying the dark imprint where Morozov's boot pressed against it. He presses a light kiss to it before he abruptly releases me. "Let's get out of here and leave this whole ordeal in the past."

He strides off without a second glance back. I move to follow him, but just then Morozov stirs with a groan. He opens his eyes, crimson eyes latching onto mine. "Do you really think I'll just let you leave with my spellbook?" he growls. "Especially now that I know just how powerful it is? I will hunt you to the end of my days."

"Yes," I say, moving closer to him. "You will. But did you really think I would let you leave here knowing the things you do about my father?"

I kneel in front of him, undoing a clasp on my ring, a gift from my father. Inside is a needle topped with a lethal poison brewed specially by our cook and personal poison expert.

Before Morozov can react, I stick him with the end of the needle.

He draws in a ragged gasp as his eyes move down. "What did you do?" he asks, but I don't need to respond because just then his whole body convulses with a shudder, followed by another one. Morozov's hand reaches vainly for his throat but there is no aiding his breathing as his throat turns to a charred black.

Vampires are immune to most poisons, but this one is made with the venom of a dragon's tooth. A very rare substance since the dragons long ago went extinct, but no ingredient is too rare for my father to find.

And the unique thing about the venom of the dragon's tooth is that it burns its victims from the inside out.

Gregos stares at me, he seems too stunned or perhaps jarred to move. I hold a finger to my lips before I push to my feet. He also knows about my father, but I can't seem to bring myself to kill him.

What was he if not an unwitting pawn in all this? He may have wanted as little a role as Wilder, besides once he was Wilder's friend, and for that, I let him live.

Even if I may someday come to regret that action.

With that taken care of, I step out of the chamber moving to catch up with Wilder and do just as he suggested. Leave this whole vampire business behind me.

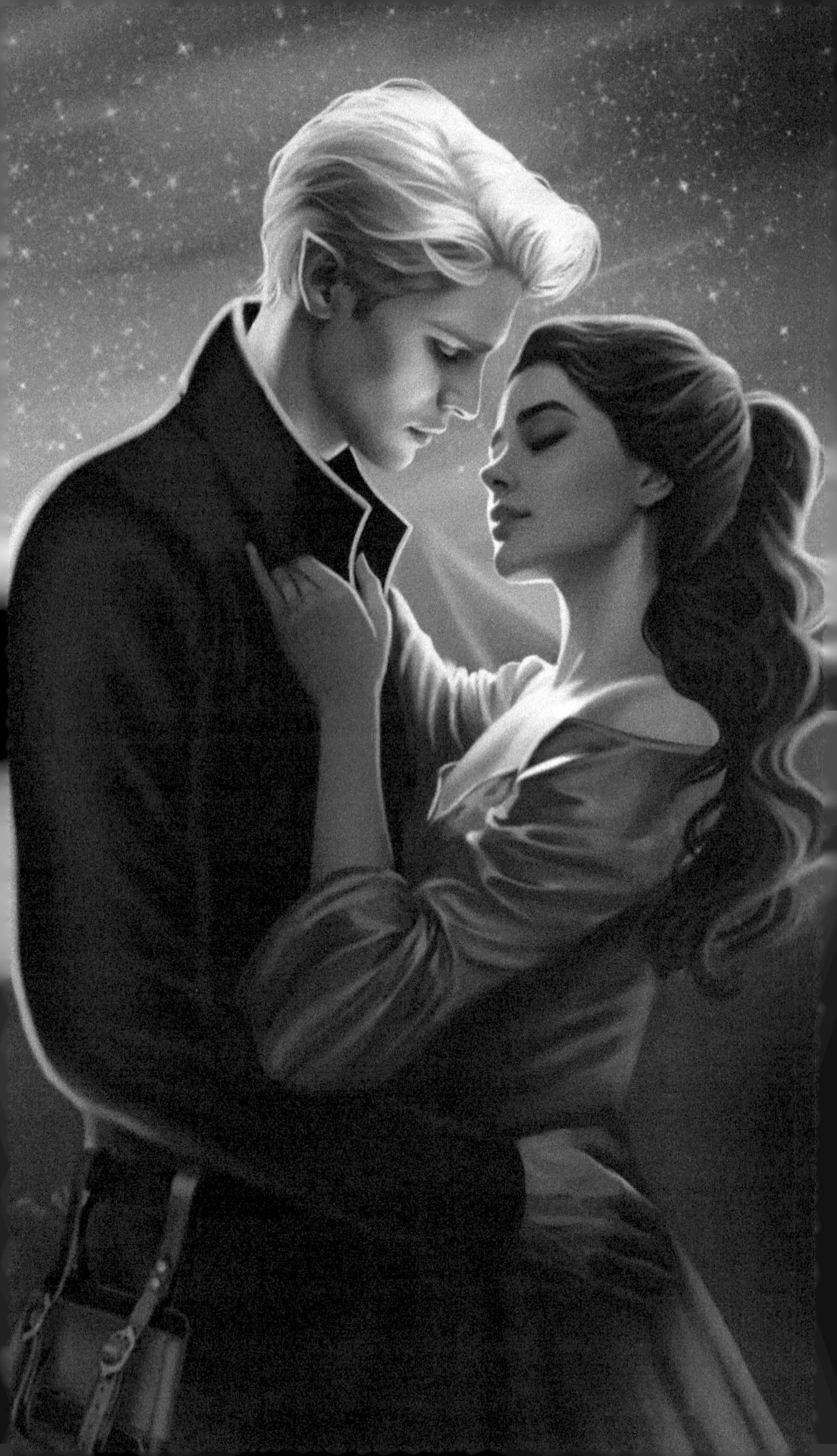

CHAPTER TWENTY-SEVEN
BRONWYN

Wilder is outside waiting for me. He is leaning on the statue of Petrov Hansimov and studying his boots. He looks up as I come up the final step.

I glance down at the book held loosely in his grasp.

"So, what now?" I ask, drawing to a halt about a foot away from him.

"I took this spell book to stop Morozov from having it," he says in a low tone. "But if I give it to you, how can I be sure that your father won't use this spellbook for evil?"

"You can't," I reply as I turn toward Wilder. "My father is not a good person. Make no mistake about that. Nor should you mistake anything I do for altruism but know that the world will not fall by our hands."

"How can I be sure?" he asks, holding the book closer to himself.

"World domination is bad for business," I reply with a shrug.

"Who are you, Bronwyn, really?"

"I'm an heir," I admit at last. "To a legacy of assassins and thieves." I pull my lip between my teeth. "I'm not the good guy and I'm sorry if you ever thought I was."

Wilder's releases a heavy breath; he works his jaw as he studies me. "Are you going to fight me for it?"

My eyes dart down to the spellbook then up to Wilder. I cross my arms tightly. "I haven't made up my mind about that yet."

He gestures to the stairs, agitated. Clearly, that wasn't what he wanted to hear. "Did you not see what I did to Morozov and my own friend? Will you really make me have to fight you off in the same way?"

I take a half step toward him but stop in case he sees my move as a threat. "I'd certainly not want to fight you for it, if that's the answer you're looking for."

He moves his hand up, running it through his hair. Finally, he nods. "I suppose it is fortuitous that I am not a good guy either. *Fine*," he draws out the word. "Eel, I'll give it to you on two conditions."

I move back, my foot meeting the cold water. I have to steady myself to keep from falling into the pool surrounding us. I had not expected him to actually give it to me. Not after learning more about who my father is, but it seems

I overestimated Wilder's desire to be a hero. "And those are?" I ask warily.

"I want to be a part of your father's business."

I can't help it; a smile of confusion takes over my expression. "What do you mean?"

He reaches out, waving his arm. "This academy is no place for me, especially without you here. I cannot go home, obviously. I cannot just *exist* in society."

"That's true, you have no applicable skills." I can't help but giggle after I say this even despite the glare he gives me.

He sniffs, offended now. "I meant because I am a vampire. But something tells me that your father's sort of... business, is perhaps the perfect place for a vampire can find a new life."

More than he realizes... not just vampires either, my father's newest assassin is a newly transformed werewolf. My father loves to collect people with special sorts of skill sets that are not available to the general populace.

"What's the second condition?" I ask.

"I want the truth out of you, Bronwyn the Eel." He pushes away from the statue and strides toward me. He doesn't stop until we are almost touching. I feel a piece of the platform flake away with the force of my leaning back and hear it splash as it lands in the pool. He presses the book into my hand, but as I grasp it, his fingers wrap around mine. His eyes hold mine spellbound and it leaves me wondering if perhaps this is also a spell found in Hansimov's book. "Do you think that it is possible that you could ever start to fall for a monster like me?"

"Oh," I breathe out. My chest feels strangely constricted as I raise my free hand up to gently trace my fingers across his cheek. Chills race up and down my spine from his cold touch. I trace over those haughty brows to the proud lines around his mouth, finally I stop my thumb resting on his lip.

"Will you still give me the book if the answer is, *no*?" My hand slides down the side of his face before resting on his shoulder.

Hurt flashes across his face, and I feel him stiffen under my grasp. "If that is the truth then yes. I will keep my end of our arrangement."

"And what will you do if the answer to that is *yes*?"

He tilts his head back in surprise. "Well, I'd kiss you, but you told me not to do that in private anymore—"

I cut him off by grasping the front of his tunic and yanking him toward me. Wilder's eyes widen in surprise, but I don't give him the chance to try to smooth talk his way out of anything. I press my lips against his.

And finally, I'm the one who kisses him. I hope this leaves him feeling just as off center and dazed as his kisses always did to me.

I pull away just enough to say, "The answer is indisputably, yes."

My mouth is so close to his that I can feel the shift as a smile breaks out across his face. He wraps his arm around my waist, pulling me into him and presses two more kisses to my lips.

"Then I think that it is time I met your father," he whispers between those kisses.

It rings out like a promise of a better life.

EPILOGUE

Lord Fraiser Zubkov was a paranoid man, but not paranoid enough to actually protect him. The vampire watched him pacing in front of the fire from the shadows of the rafters of Fraiser's ostentatious manor.

It was no easy feat finding a way in, especially since he was specifically asked not to kill anyone, but if there was one thing that Elwis the Eel loved, it was a challenge.

Moving silently, as if he was one with the shadows, Elwis dropped to the ground. He leaned against the pillar and cleared his throat.

Fraiser jumped, whirling as he scanned the room. However, with Elwis's dark clothing and hair, he blended perfectly into the shadows, so Fraiser had to scan the room twice before he saw him.

"Who are you?" Fraiser demanded, his hand straying to the dagger at his side. It was ornate, probably just for show.

"I'm just a messenger. There's no need to be afraid, I was *asked* not to kill you, and at the moment. I'm feeling generous."

Elwis strode forward, allowing the shadows around him to melt away, revealing his full stature. As a Lower Elf, he towered over the Lowlander lordling. "I am here to tell you not to go looking for your son. He is safe and he is far from you, that's all that matters, isn't it?"

Fraiser swallowed, fury taking over his expression finally showing some backbone. "How dare you come into my home and tell me what I can or cannot do about my son. I demand to know who you are and where Wilder is."

In the blink of an eye, Elwis had unsheathed his dagger and used his sorcery to control it. It flew across the room, hovering only an inch from the lord's face. Elwis moved his finger back and forth and the dagger followed suit. "Tsk tsk, I don't take well to demands. And secondly, that message comes from your son. He is the one that requested I not kill you. He said, *not even a scar*. If you want me to respect his wishes, I suggest that you do the same."

Elwis strode toward the window, it was the third story. He paused on the ledge, turning to where the lord stood, white as a sheet with the dagger still suspended in front of him. Elwis held out his hand and the dagger flew back into it. "I'll be keeping a close eye on you, Zubkov. If I see anything I don't like, I will return. And I won't be nearly as civil."

He stepped out the window, however before gravity could yank him down, a vine that had been growing along the side of the house wrapping around his waist and bringing him carefully to the ground.

Truthfully, this visit to Fraiser was a waste, and he would have rather been able to just kill him and be done with it, but Wilder had begged him. Elwis liked this Wilder boy. With him already being a vampire, it will make Bronwyn's transition easier when she finally chose to embrace the gift of the night. And someday, Wilder will inherit an impressive family fortune–even if he wouldn't let Elwis kill his father and take it now.

Elwis could work with that.

Besides, the boy was instrumental in getting the spellbook, or so Bronwyn claimed. She seemed to be trying to paint Wilder in the best light. Elwis found that so quaint. Ah, young love... he remembered his courting of Vala. He had thought the world of her back then, and it was very clear that Bronwyn had the same stars in her eyes.

No matter how large of a role the boy played, his beautiful Bronwyn had done well, and now he had the personal spell tome of one of the most powerful magickers of all time in his possession.

One down, only three more to go.

And he just so happened to have finally uncovered the location of the next one through the lineage of the next founder of the academy. Boris the Conjurer.

This looked like a job for his darling Natasya.

Afterword

Bronwyn and Wilder **will** return.

Don't miss Natasya's story in...
This Hollow Heart
A Legend of Sleepy Hollow Retelling
Coming This Fall

MORE STORIES FROM RUSKHAZAR

Don't Miss These Other Books Set in Ruskhazar

Between Gods and Demigods (*Rage Like the Gods,* book 0.5)
Rage Like the Gods (*Rage Like the Gods,* book one)
A Tale of Gods and Glory
The Gods Created Monsters (*What the Gods Did,* book one)

ACKNOWLEDGEMENTS

I reach the end of a book but find the hardest words to say are the final two: thank you. Not because I'm impassionate about it. No, it's quite the opposite. I'm so full of gratitude that I don't even know where to start or how to express it, but perhaps the easiest way is to say it simply. So here it is. Thank you.

Thank you to the lovely ladies I published this with: Jes, Stephanie, Jessica, and Megan. You are the best author friends a gal could ask for and I'm so happy to have been able to publish another series with you.

To my family for your constant support along the way and eye rolls when I said I was making characters inspired by my love for Dramione.

To my readers for taking this plunge and starting on another adventure with me. I hope you enjoyed the ride cause it's not quite over yet...

To my dragons for being the most amazing street team ever.

To my editor Eve for the wonderful work that you did. To Grace Morris and Sarah Ryder, my typo hunters.

To my cover designers Saint Jupiter and Lauren for everything that you did to bring my ideas to life. And to Maddy for the gorgeous character illustrations of Bronwyn and Wilder. And to Chaim for the gorgeous map.

To Jesus for *everything*.

ALSO BY NICKI CHAPELWAY

Of Gold and Iron (*The Of Dreams and Nightmares trilogy*, book one)
Of Stars and Shadows (*The Of Dreams and Nightmares trilogy*, book two)
Of Dawn and Fire (*The Of Dreams and Nightmares trilogy*, book three)

Bound by Knighthood

An Apprentice of Death (*An Apprentice of Death*, book one)
A House of Blood (*And Apprentice of Death*, book two)

A Winter Grim and Lonely (*Winter Cursed*, book 0.5)
Winter Cursed (*Winter Cursed*, book one)
A Winter Dark and Deadly (*Winter Cursed*, book two)

Harbinger of the End: A Tale of Loki and Sigyn

And They All Bow Down

A Week of Werewolves, Faeries, and Fancy Dresses (*My Time in Amar*, book one)
A Time of Trepidation, Pirates, and Lost Princesses (*My Time in Amar*, book two)
A Season of Subterfuge, Courtiers, and War Councils (*My Time in Amar*, book three)

A Certain Sort of Madness (*Return to Amar*, book one)
A Matter of Curiosity (Return to Amar, book two)

OF SEAS AND TIDES

Trapped by Pirates — Stephanie BwaBwa
Trapped by Magic — Nicki Chapelway
Trapped by Neverland — Megan Charlie
Trapped by Claws — Jessica M. Butler
Trapped by Vengeance — Jes Drew

Milton Keynes UK
Ingram Content Group UK Ltd.
UKHW051945240624
444478UK00015BA/89/J